Further Praise

ALLAN GURC

and his

LOCAL SOULS

"Witty and soulful. . . . Gurganus manages the neat hat trick of blending the stuff of everyday life with Faulkner-ian gothic and Chekhov-ian soul-searching, all told in assured language that resounds, throughout all three novellas, in artfully placed sententiae. . . . [T]he novellas have a conversational tone and easy manner that are testimony to the author's craftsmanship."

Kirkus Reviews, starred review

"Sixty years ago, Lionel Trilling rejected the idea that Sherwood Anderson could ever be a major writer, accusing him of vaporous sentimentality. His one truth, though, if it is taken out of Anderson's hands, remains a firm truth: 'The small legitimate existence, so necessary for the majority of men to achieve, is in our age so very hard, so nearly impossible, for them to achieve.' In Allan Gurganus's fiction, though, there is no sentimentalizing over life's hardness, perhaps because more of his men and women achieve a legitimate existence than is usual in contemporary American fiction."

—D. G. Myers, *Barnes & Noble Review*

"As Thomas Mallon noted in *The New Yorker*, in an age of literary minimalists, Gurganus stands as a Baroque aristocrat. His long, ruminative sentences, trailing dependent clauses, read like some collaboration between William Faulkner and

Henry James. . . . Through it all, Gurganus is hypersensitive to the nuances of class and clan in the small-town South. . . . From the coming of the Yankees to the malling of the bypasses and the withering of downtowns to security that vanished with the winds of Floyd and the fires of 9/11, *Local Souls* is a fine barometric charting of where we were and how we are now."

—Ben Steelman, *StarNews*

"It's been 12 years since Gurganus last published a full-length work—but if there remains any doubt of his literary greatness, his fifth book, *Local Souls*, should put it to rest forever. . . . A tour de force in the tradition of Hawthorne. It shows that Gurganus's vast creative and imaginative powers, still rooted in the local, are increasingly universal in scope and effect. The book is an expansive work of love. . . . Gurganus moves beyond [Sherwood] Anderson and even Faulkner in calling into question the very notion of 'inappropriate': the emotional misalignments in his fiction feel both understandable and familiar. Like Chekhov and Cheever before him, Gurganus registers an enormous amount of compassion for the characters he holds to the fire."

—Jamie Quatro, *New York Times Book Review*

"Despite his Iowa M.F.A., Gurganus writes novels and short stories that don't follow the usual workshop rule to show instead of tell. Nor do they break it any simple way. . . . The first-person voice's capacity for lifelikeness and oral illusion has been Gurganus's great Southern storytelling inheritance. . . . *Local Souls* stays true to its author's vocal aesthetic."

—Thomas Mallon, *The New Yorker*

"The name Allan Gurganus . . . is virtually synonymous with Southern lit. . . . Throughout all these stories, the characters' doubts about themselves and their world take them on a meandering route through life that, in the Southern way, emulates politeness but masks deeper anxieties and raises questions about their place as individuals and as parts of a culture that teeters on a fault line perpetually threatening to crack wide open."

—Michelle Moriarity Witt, *News & Observer*

"Gurganus [is] fearfully gifted. . . . The gem of *Local Souls* is the gorgeous 'Decoy,' in which Gurganus removes the gloves and delivers the literary equivalent of a bare-knuckled knockout. 'Decoy' is so good that you want to lob all sorts of adjectives its way: warm, humane, profound, sagacious, hilarious, nostalgic, and incisive. . . . The last pages of *Local Souls* prove once again that there is no writer alive quite like Allan Gurganus."

—Laura Albritton, *Miami Herald*

"Allan Gurganus proves once again that small-town life in the New South can be as tragic and twisted as anything out of an ancient Greek playbook. . . . The chatty, roundabout storytelling, the wicked humor and sense of the absurd often disguise the gravity of these investigations into life's tendency to 'retract its promise overnight,' to 'become a vale of tears breaking over you in sudden lashing.' Hidden above the safe confines of the Falls, Zeus readies his lightning bolts."

—Gina Webb, *Atlanta Journal-Constitution*

"A serious and important American writer—his work has meant a lot to me over time. . . . [I]t's good to have him back after a long absence."

—Dwight Garner, *New York Times*

"How refreshing to come across art that moves along humorously and scarily beneath our habitual presentations of self in everyday life. Gurganus offers an antidote to the market place's mass message and massage, keeps our attention on local souls—on people who live next door, especially if you're from a small Southern town like the fictional one that is the central locale of each of these novellas, as well as many Gurganus stories."

—Clyde Edgerton, *Garden and Gun*

"[*Local Souls*] is an astounding testament to Gurganus's narrative vibrancy, faultless plotting, and Everyman/mythic vision. . . . [He is] one of the most exciting fiction writers alive. . . . Of living novelists in English, only Martin Amis and Cormac McCarthy can match Gurganus's pyrotechnical aptitude for language, for forging a verbiage both rapturous and exact. He's categorically incapable of crafting a dull sentence."

—William Giraldi, *Oxford American*

"In this first work in 12 years, Gurganus offers three luscious, perceptively written pieces, each as rich as any full-length novel and together exploring the depth of our connections. . . . In all three novellas, there's a pervasive sense of the power of community expectations and the question of whether we can challenge fate. . . . These pieces are so fresh and real that the reader has the sense of walking through a dissolving plate-glass window straight into the lives of the characters. Highly recommended."

—*Library Journal*, starred review

"Thoroughly enjoyable. . . . Here are finely rendered portraits— and, behind the faces, fascinating stories. Listen to the voices, so pitch perfect, the words, oh so readable. And Falls, home to the fallen; it's on the map. Come visit."

—Tom Lavoie, Shelf Awareness

"Here's something to celebrate: Gurganus is publishing his first work in over a decade, and the setting is Falls, NC, the mythic town that serves as the setting of his first novel, the knockout *Oldest Living Confederate Widow Tells All.* . . . Expect to hear lots about this book."

—*Library Journal*

DECOY

DECOY

A NOVELLA

Allan Gurganus

LIVERIGHT PUBLISHING CORPORATION

A DIVISION OF W. W. NORTON & COMPANY

NEW YORK • LONDON

For information about permission to reproduce selections from this book,
write to Permissions, Liveright Publishing Corporation,
a division of W. W. Norton & Company, Inc.,
500 Fifth Avenue, New York, NY 10110

For information about special discounts for bulk purchases,
please contact W. W. Norton Special Sales at
specialsales@wwnorton.com or 800-233-4830

Manufacturing by RR Donnelley, Harrisonburg, VA
Book design by JAM Design
Production manager: Beth Steidle

Library of Congress Cataloging-in-Publication Data

Gurganus, Allan, 1947–
Decoy : a novella / Allan Gurganus.
pages cm
ISBN 978-1-63149-025-5 (pbk.)
I. Title.
PS3557.U814D33 2015
813'.54—dc23

2015000307

Liveright Publishing Corporation, 500 Fifth Avenue, New York, N.Y. 10110
www.wwnorton.com

W. W. Norton & Company Ltd., Castle House, 75/76 Wells Street, London W1T 3QT

1 2 3 4 5 6 7 8 9 0

For Paul Taylor

DECOY

BOOK ONE
B.C.

Night comes down so hard around my little boat. At last one oar strikes the floating trophy. I've hunted this since dusk. It has been tangled in a nest of reeds offshore. Blind, I finally reach for it two-handed. How easily and wet it comes to me. The carving, smoothed, is cold as silver. Darkness helps me feel both sides' engraving.

With this small idol in my lap, I am free to paddle any-where, to simply drift. Sunset's many reds have dyed themselves one black. Over water, over me, stars brighten till they each have fur. Now my boat will likely swerve beyond the shore-line's homey docks. Current soon enough should pull me out to sea. Oh, I know the odds.

But, with this onboard—hand-carved to represent me—I feel tallied.

Described, I can risk everything.

I am at last a man accompanied.

OUR HOUSES STILL looked beautiful to us.

Everybody here, black and white, inherited a little something. Right away we'd reinvest.

Many bright people—born in Falls, NC—left home early. Else-where they do get famous faster. Still, we'd brag, "Sat behind me in third grade. Borrowed notebook paper, daily." The world press pre-fers such city celebrities. But, even now, I think the Lord is quickest to forgive us local souls.

We Bible believers—too punctual—were always likeliest to stay. Falls, with thirteen more churches than car dealerships, wants its citizens optimistic if stationary. Was it even our choice? Hadn't our temperaments decided? Or getting deeded land that, being highly-local, also stayed. If a person doesn't fight gravity, it wants you right where you *have* been.

Our Falls stands thirty miles from other towns. Once renowned for our tobacco auctions, we've lived to hear ourselves called "the Smoking Section." Being a farm-sized city-state, we do take good care of us. We're rarely unintentionally rude. My smart wife says to say: We still tend to worship our doctors and diagnose our preachers.

We've pledged allegiance to what my young daughter called, "one nation, under God, in the visible." Quick to smile "Prettiest morning ever!" we hide our doubts through most of each day's cocktail hour.

And yet, till right here recently, we hadn't really known dying meant us.

AROUND HERE WE'RE kind of funny about our doctors. Since Falls lies below sea level, we like medical heroics of a towering kind. We favor extreme measures to keep us alive. The farther your hometown gets stuck off by itself, the more faith you'll put into your main medicine man. (If God's some sort of doctor, must be quite the general practitioner!)

We figure: if our physician is a man *good* enough, he'll keep our deaths at bay a couple extra years. (And if yours played college basketball, stands six-something, won fellowships to Davidson then Yale? Hell, that's worth at least a six-month bonus!)

Weekends before the trouble, people entertained. You pretty much had to. House-proud, flirtatious, leading couples took turns. We liked our martinis as dry as possible; we preferred our sex not. Sex here meant mostly married sex—but that was okay.

Party invitations? answered one day after mailing. And when your son fell off his bike three blocks from home? another adult would dash out, Band-Aid his scrape, phone you reassurance, praising Billy's coloring and manners. Heaven and Hell must share a pretty violent border. Canyon fires, screaming refugees. But here? At our river's edge? the Last Judgment seemed other people's visa problem.

Falls' 6,803 souls felt known for generations by both first-and-last names. Our homes, remodeled, looked even better to us. Not quite a heaven? but surely zoned to banish eyesore hell. And folks that left at age eighteen—even ones now well-known artists in New York— you think they're a bit happier?

Those of us who stuck by Falls, we sometimes fear we've fallen off the big-time honor-roll. And yet, our town—if on certain days a letdown—landed intact, nicely right-side-up beside the still waters. Till right here lately, we who stayed, stayed mostly cozy.

Between hot-cold extremes, you'll sometimes get this bonus. The one honeyed crease, sweet river-basin cleavage. The open sesame nuzzle-spot no newcomer ever finds.

OURS BEING A farm-town, we idolize those experts most hands-on. So when our beloved general practitioner announced he'd finally retire, neighbors threw Doc Roper forty tribute bashes. Roper? the last physician who forgot to send your annual bill. No wonder folks baked "farewell" cakes from scratch. (One was shaped like a bone-saw! That drunk, people ate it anyway.)

Ask anybody. Falls' best neighborhood? Riverside. The one guide-book calls it "most desirable." Finer homes got built along our placid waterway, the River Lithium; it somehow always cheered us, even its mists. We'd lucked out—living in earshot of water's daily moods, annual duck migrations. And Doc Roper tended our twelve square blocks and more. He was never a licensed surgeon. But lank at seventy, everybody's family physician still wielded his knife like some artist.

"New starter cyst back here, Bill. Shall we just get it *now*?" And Roper—as mild as tall behind you—described how, this Thanksgiving, his Marge would be serving duck, not turkey. Six canvasbacks he'd bagged at sunrise on the Carolina coast. "There," he touched your shoulder. "Good as new." And your surgery, affordable, was behind you.

One neighbor, still loyal to that discredited Dr. Dennis S—, grumbled about the *Herald-Traveler*'s Roper issue. A whole insert devoted to Doc's bowing out. "Any man that admired must be holding stuff back." But *what?* The Ropers' river place stood just opposite Janet's and mine. Our teak decks plateaued at one level these forty years; any secret there must sure be sealed watertight. To date, Doc's life appeared driven, rangy, civic. That's why retirement might prove his Waterloo. We worried for him, going forward. And, incidentally, for us here, left behind.

He'd grown up local but more on Riverside's raggedy south edge. A few 1940s Colonials but mostly ugly yellow rentals. His handsome parents paid their country club dues with the month-end strain of poor folks tithing. Even before Roper left for scholarships at Davidson before Yale Med School, classmates dubbed him *Doc.* (What if kids had called him *Preacher?* Would he then have come clear home to heal our spirits?) He suffered a most ladylike first name: "Marion." Seeing the boy's kindness and smarts, pals upgraded him in fifth grade. Boneless *Marion* became our useful *Doc.*

HIS WHOLE LAST duty-month got spoiled by Falls' champagne and testimonials. Hating full-frontal praise, any overpayment, Roper kept studying the silver buckle of his wristwatch-band. The emcee laughed, "Now chime in, folks. Watch him blush, today-only he's our sitting duck."

Recovered patients toasted him. A wheelchair traffic jam at Lane's End Rest Home. His Tex-Mex office-cleaning crew brought Roper home-brewed beer and a mariachi band of brothers-in-law. Doc's Sherlock diagnoses got described but only after many revolting symptoms. Folks recalled how, new to local practice, Roper had accepted barter.

In those days, he couldn't bear to turn away country people like my ailing dad and me. Back then Roper looked to be just one more serious Yalie. But his card-playing father, so rarely rich, had taught him what it meant to live on cocktail crackers. The neighbors guessed and fed the boy. Doc always talked easily with black folks who worked tobacco. So, in exchange for services, he started by accepting firewood, motorboat tune-ups for life. Tomatoes left on his new white station wagon's roof liquefied by noon, ruining the paint job.

One thing wrong with Doc, there seemed so little "off." The man gave us admitted sinners insufficient human traction. Not one comic vice, no obsessive hobbies. Wouldn't time reverse that? Might not leisure do him in? Why stop working anyway? "If you ain't broke, don't quit *fix*ing . . . us!" one tipsy lady-partier blurted. Others called his stiffing us a matter of life and death. Silent, I only nodded.

From my farm-born father, I'd inherited a punk heart and the disease as scary as its name, *familial hypercholesterolemia.* Your LDL- and HDL-count lives up in the three- and four-hundreds. No "countervailing agent" countervails. Your heart keeps trying to become a mineral. Only neighbor Roper has eased me through three, count them, full-blown attacks. "What will we do with*out* him?" people asked at church and in checkout lines. Me, I could only shrug. Didn't his sailing straight into the sunset leave my rowboat capsized just offshore? —Still, I had to wish him well.

Even so, rule one: *Make sure your favorite family doctor is at least a decade-and-a-half your* junior.

OUR NEIGHBORHOOD CURVES along one slow tea-colored tributary. The more feet of waterfront your fine home claims, the more you likely paid. Serious establishments come with narrow beaches (white sand bought by the truckload). Diving platforms float mid-Lithium. The handrails of our docks have cup-rests cut right in. Suitable to hold a dozen friends' gins and t's.

Our major fears, they've all been engineered around. Maybe that's why country people after church drove clear to town to stare across lawns of The River Road. Family money allows a margin of safety. However many inches. What scared us worst? our kids or grandkids drowning. (Neighbors' sons—undergrads home from Vanderbilt or Sewanee—could still earn three grand a summer improving the breaststrokes of little juniors next door.)

SHOULDN'T THOSE OF us who'd stayed Falls' guardians be offered combat pay? Might not the damage done us on-duty be prorated to reflect those risks knowingly assumed? (I once sold insurance.) We stayed home to avoid danger but it had our home addresses. My wife says my four-square face should be stamped PAYS HIS PROPERTY TAXES EARLY. But maybe the harder you avoid a thing, the greater its impact incoming?

For those now-famous friends who'd abandoned Falls early, what we just survived—without them—might be the only reason we'd still interest them.

2

FOR EACH OF Doc Roper's retirement buffets, you could name the injury that inspired it: he had stitched shut the forehead of a child who somehow rammed his trike through Grandmother's patio plate-glass. And if our teen daughter (speaking generally here) suddenly found herself in the family way, our general practitioner never *took care* of her himself; but Doc was sure to know the best man in Durham—who might just know somebody helpful.

"What in hell will you *do* all day?" neighbors asked at Roper's fourth surprise barbeque. Fellows sounded interested if irked. Others, close to ending their own work-years, felt scared of being idled. Then here came Doc—self-employed, braving that, eased-out only by himself and the wife.

"Oh, boys," he smiled at deacon faces fifteen years ago, "something'll bob up. My kids gave me an Apple laptop, still in its crate somewhere. Our two in grad school sound scared I might come north, try taking classes with them. Funny, I *do* feel ready to finally become a good student! Last time, looks like I coasted on my . . . well, on my I-don't-know-what! Luck? Always have hated *sit*ting. Next week Marge here has us flying to Bermuda for twenty-one whole days. —

Right, my li'l Margie? Lady put her foot down. Says she's not having our usual weekend with me hooked to patients or the doggone phone. After that, we'll see . . ."

People said it was an American tragedy. He knew so much. And about us! Our septic innards, our secret chin-lifts, our actual alcohol intake in liters-per-day. Plus Doc never snitched. You could tell him anything, if you could only think something *up*!

Made you wish science would hurry. Young geniuses should mastermind a brain-transplant procedure. When his time came, imagine downloading Roper's gray matter into some strong new pink intern!

Where is it written that a sane, vigorous man of seventy has to pack it in?

Doc's yellow hair had turned all white at age thirty; that set him apart somehow, a person sanitized if not quite priestly. He'd kept himself good and trim. Swam in our river almost daily just at dawn. Still jogged, shirtless. True, while running Doc's torso was maybe more in motion than a man of forty's. But, once stopped, everything rose up near where it'd started. He was just ten years my senior, as I likely already said. On myself, I've lately noticed how soon male-tenderloin can texture toward being beef jerky. At best!

You'd often spy him at the club, fitting in a fast nine holes, if rarely played with the same duffers. He was too smart to be only perfect as you heard. It must get old, staying that observed, admired. Some days, yeah, he could act kind of testy. His jokes could have flint in them. If your accident-prone child lay bleeding on his exam table, some of Doc's quips truly cut.

"Bill?" Roper spoke (to me) over my young son's compound fracture, "Bill, can't you help your Billy boy here find any *high*er trees to fall out of? Hasn't missed many in this county—now, have you, pal?" Ha *ha*. You see?

Still, he was most everybody's doctor. The competition wasn't, and his waiting room was a salad bar of classes, races. Curious, Roper's bills seemed to reach richer clients quickest and give the poorer recovery-time. Need be, he'd pass you on to specialists. Doc said he owed me a bit extra: how my own dad had perished in his care, in our company. So I've been Roper's patient-dependent for, what? going on forty years be July tenth. I've counted on our standing weekly appointment, sunup Monday mornings. Had my own in-office coffee mug, a gift from Roper's tough-talking nurses. Blanche, Sandy, and the other Sandy.

SOMETIMES ENTERING OUR town's country club I still worry I'm dressed goofy. These old tennis shoes too grass-stained? Slightly sunburned, don't I look more a rural Baptist than any chess-playing Episcopalian? But I have belonged here on a donated legacy-membership for five decades! When will I *not* feel guest-on-approval? Blame our family's slipping into Falls so late. We barely made the broad-jump from clay tobacco fields to red clay courts. And then only thanks to Dad's strange good fortune.

Riverside's tulip poplars and water-dipping willows can keep our oasis fifteen degrees cooler than bordering farmland. My poppa, though born out there in sun-glare, loved hidden Riverside nearly to the point of being pagan. By June, fields the boy plowed were sun-blasted toward ceramic. Just to carve down in and plant your seed was about like breaking plates.

Pop bragged he'd got born self-employed, lived to be indentured. Luck only came to Pop once he retired. If Doc Roper's parents stayed the best-looking fox-trotters nearest the bandstand at the club, my dad barely glimpsed membership's brick fortress, and then only over a hedge, from a public road.

"Red" Mabry was the son of a mule-driving tenant farmer from way on out in Person County. If his borrowed truck had not broken down he might never have discovered Falls' quietest neighborhood. Red had been driving since age nine. Was then he finally grew tall enough to dance while standing on his left leg, his right one operating gas or brake as he clung to the wheel.

Stranded along The River Road, awaiting some jackleg mechanic,

Red wandered off into greenest luxury. (He later admitted he'd been seeking some nice quiet bush to pee on. But rich folks' bushes were all trimmed up to look like man-sized chess pieces that seemed likely to pee right back at you.) Gardening crews had come at sunrise and left by 8 a.m. Like dew itself, maintenance refreshed then disappeared. The River Road in early June was all lipstick tulips against emerald lawns.

I picture little Mabry—denim coveralls, red hair looking like his one cash crop, probably openmouthed with pleasure. He finally saw how industrial wealth, left alone amid its own upholstery, can choose to live. In 1938 no gates or guards kept anybody out.

This son of sharecropping had never glimpsed lawns acres wide. Of no silage value. Hell, you couldn't even bail stuff this short to feed your poppa's cattle. Grass here meant to be a kind of moat. It would keep your white house hid-back awninged in blue eye shadow. A row of riverside homes looked shapely yet hard to please. They were bay-windowed big-fronted as Miss Mae West. Like Mae, they posed uphill, terraced onto hips, expecting farm boy stares, their stances still jack-hammer-resistant.

Young Red noted folks' driveways flagstoned then bar-bent U-shaped. One brand-new canary-yellow LaSalle convertible sat parked out front, keys left right in it! That summer day, owing to a busted axle, Red Mabry became another teen who'd fallen hard. Got his heart set, see. Not on some hellion Zelda debutante, thank God; fixed more on a neighborhood called "highly desirable." Our hick was hooked on professional lawn care in that age of bamboo rakes before leaf-blowers; kid got fixed on having a third story set cute as a sailor-girl's cap atop your regular roof. Mabry hoped to someday spring himself (and any future kin) from sharecropper's usual, a rabbit-box of country shack.

My dad, not a little bowlegged, had been called "Red" since the midwife's first alarmed sight of him. Given his eighth-grade education, considering his poor health, the little fellow's leap to being someone "town" was probably impossible.

DR. ROPER, BEING fifty, but still looking thirty-eight, happened to be jogging past a kids' swimming party. He heard screams from the Bixby twins' sixth birthday. As neighbors, Janet and I had just popped in for cake. I became one of five men who waded out and found the little brothers' cooling bodies. We laid them face-up onshore as Doc, dropping to his knees, barked, "Align. Heads. Please." See, instead of wedging himself between them—where he must do lateral twists, wasting time—he knew to kneel up by their droopy noggins. Doc pulled both those heads onto his lap and bent across them from above. Shirtless himself, he huffed and heaved his air into our identical dead. A feeding, he pressed the Bixbys' skulls so close together Roper seemed to pant into a single mouth.

Boys had plunged under river-water hand-in-hand trying some weird twins' pact or dare. Now Doc exhaled into Timmy, then Tommy, alternating. We all stood crying, holding on to one another. Three women supported the young mother. In minutes Tim coughed a quart of the River Lithium; then Tom sat up and pointed at his brother. He accused the other of breathing first, ruining the "speriment." Roper laughed, shook his head. "What exactly was your *plan*, boys?"

All of us, shaken, went direct from tears to cackling. Kids' beautiful mother felt so grateful, so stunned at losing then regaining them, she—quiet, hysterical—knelt beside Doc and offered him . . . a kiss, openmouthed, the works. This happened in June and Katie Bixby filled out her Jantzen one-piece pretty good. All she could think to give Roper was herself. His own wife Marge had just come running, hearing shouts. Margie stood not ten feet off when Doc told Mrs. Bixby, "Thanks, dear girl, but you're in shock. Y'owe me nothing. Go take yourself a goodly snort of brandy. Then stick these daredevils in a long, hot bubble bath—well-monitored, y' hear?"

ROPER'S FATHER HAD it bad for gambling. Dapper fellow, looked like he owned Shell Oil while goading any shoeshine boy to wager:

"Freddy, tell me, since you know a lot. How late *you* figure today's freight train's running?" Neighbors swore that one midnight Roper, Sr., came home naked, shoeless, wearing just a hotel blanket. Also missing, the family Chrysler. His poor wife had to go out and pay the cab. Drake Roper's 007 manner got him into those very club games he could least afford.

And Doc's mom? A true beauty forced to teach local brats piano. We'd hear her tapping out our five-eight time, seated behind the bench where we slaved over our Czerny; we'd hear Mrs. Roper toy with her pearls, turn toward the window, sigh a lot.

DOC'S OWN GROWING kids often heard from townsfolk how fortunate they were. They'd glaze right over, snort at each other. You sensed the dad must've been pretty darn human, once finally home at seven p.m. Controlling maybe? Cold? You could only guess which usual problem was his.

Roper's son and daughter were loyal enough never to say one thing against him, at least nothing you could quote. They'd been shipped early off to Northern prep schools (as if to help them keep Dad's secrets). The daughter was now big into African-American art history; the son at Harvard, I think in the divinity-theology line. Blond lookers, both of them. We rarely saw them, even certain Thanksgivings. Sad that no new young Dr. Roper would be rushing south to try replacing him.

Though one decade older than I, Doc had a better memory. In his office, he recalled verbatim my last year's wavering blood work. At his fingertips my Dow Jones good cholesterol gone bad. Man never needed to speed-read the fat manila folder Nurse Blanche left opened for him every Monday anyway.

OUR PART OF North Carolina is so darned flat we'll do most anything to stir up some variety. Mystery, please. If not adultery, how about a hill? Oh, to have experienced some cloud-high risks. We'd even court a few pit-of-hell lows. —Results? Mostly golf courses.

The berg nearest ours named itself for a pile of mill-side stones, "Rocky Mound." Didn't that sound too bland to merit a post office? So town fathers upscaled it to: "Rocky Moun-*t*." One letter seemed to shoot the town hundreds of feet above sea-level. And us? We've always had this placid river chockablock with Ice Age stones. So, those few jagged rocks that babbled audibly? we upgraded. To a word nearly-Niagaran: "Falls"!

Tourists ask to see our waterfalls. Our what?

Residents couldn't bear to call themselves the "Fallsites." (Didn't that sound like some minor form of feldspar, like the word *falsies?*) That's when our early nineteenth century membership had several drinks and dubbed itself "the Fallen."

"How long have you been among the Fallen, or were your people born that way?"

MY DAD STUCK out eighth grade till Christmas vacation. After that, Red hammered his way to being a contractor miles from Falls. County jobs proved spotty, as rural pay was poor. Still, folks trusted him on sight. Mabry gave honest estimates, simply said what he meant. That came out surprising, funny, finally kind of rare. Inheriting the weak heart that'd killed his dad, he stayed down nearly-child-sized. He had to hire subcontractors, older, able-bodied men. And yet, he chose to marry the prettiest honor student from a one-room crossroads school. Nine months later to the day, they welcomed their towheaded baby, me. And Red Mabry—officially an invalid, exempt from soldiering in WWII—somehow supported us.

He swore our finally getting into Falls was God apologizing. For making our family tradition be terrible health. Red had strict doctors' orders to never lift a tool heavier than his clipboard and, yes, okay, its pen.

His very ears were freckled like concert tickets punch-holed. His cracked grin made you laugh at, alongside, then with it. The man pretty much radiated enthusiasm. For belief, most any belief. Faith in his own faith and others'. Love is one thing. Red's belief, being general and village-sized, seemed less private and selfish than romance. A heart in trade. A heart like some shop sign hung right out front.

WHILE ROPER'S PARENTS played tourney bridge or spiral-peeled lemon zests for drinks, my dad and mom still rocked me on the porch of our tin-roofed farmhouse. They took turns fanning yellow jackets off baby-me as Red talked a blue streak about Falls' tree cover. "Streets like 'forest glades,' the best blocks." His county tone could swan-dive up into an Irish dreamer's. Pop got crushes on certain words. "Glade," "mitered" and "half-timbered Tudor" each held pride-of-place there for a while.

Red swore that Riverside's constant sound of flowing water would cool us off and heal us up. Red rattled on about the charm of rich people generally: how they had doctors as good as any U.S. president's; how they could make just some weekday the occasion for a party worth uncounted shrimp platters, real Chinese lanterns. Dad swore that even Falls' oldest sickest rich folks, why, they never looked near so ham-colored, sweaty, or plain-bad as his many heavyset cousins out this way.

Dad had memorized street numbers along The River Road, near-catechism. He mapped so much about which fine family lived where since when. In my later decades spent among the Fallen, Red's start-up bloodline flowchart proved infallible. It saved me much embarrassment among cousins. Except for me, they all were. Cousins. One town girl was named Whitson Whitson and her brother bled.

If my dad had to die early, he got lots done beforehand. Our first week in Falls, Red started hunting medical help for the both of us. Pop found two town doctors far superior to a near-veterinarian who'd treated us as full-fledged members of the rural poor. Then Dad sought even better care as far away as a new college hospital over in Greenville.

Finally internist-generalist Roper returned to his hometown. There was a party in honor of that, too. He'd just finished at New

Haven. At last, with this new-minted grad just turned twenty nine, with me a shy nineteen, with Dad one feisty if twisted forty-seven, Doc accepted us as clients. Then, slower, Roper took us up as friends. He was the first to understand, then explain, what-all was wrong with us. Nobody till then could say what we *had*.

Past my condition, I never understood Roper's own. Why, with his skill and looks and Yale MD, come back to Falls? Was that not a relapse?

And why would such a one *stay*?

3

FORTY YEARS AFTER signing on as Dad's doctor and mine, after all those years of human holding and mending, Roper folded. He had given Falls a full six months' notice. Claimed his wife had made him do it. "Marge showed me the kitchen calendar and asked if I recognized one date and when I told her I'd turn seventy then she said it'd also be the day she got me back. 'Patience finally wins out over patients.' So be it. Marge has asked for so little." Still, when it hit, his disappearance felt overnight. The last appointments were completed (except last stragglers bearing cookies, photographs).

The notice Scotch-taped to his locked office door was just a piece of typing paper handwritten by Doc's head nurse:

> *Will no longer be seeing patients as of today, folks. Sorry. It has sure been real.*

Roper sold his local practice to a recent Emory grad. That poor kid had his work cut out for him. Doc acted unsentimental. Every grocery aisle held damp-eyed wheezy well-wishers trying not to show him their new rash. How could any future avocation compete? What'd ever be alive and grimly funny as our community these last four decades?

If he took to his rocking chair, he'd surely sit there missing office hours crowded with our small-beer woes and charms. Looking back, maybe we all felt a little jealous . . . of whatever he'd take up next. His clearing out made us feel we'd been ditched. We might all be his plain steadying first spouse, the gal who slaved at catering to put her go-to guy through med school.

Though widely admired, Roper was odd in having no one best friend. Never even seemed to *miss* one. (Were there a few leading candidates? Oh, sure. His cross-the-way neighbor, yours truly, lived, watchful, among them.) Sure, I'd have "hung with him," as our grandkids said till recently. But from boyhood up, solitude appeared a part of Roper's plan. His dad had been a much-watched loner forever waiting for some CIA assignment or midnight game. And our doctor had just such stand-apart power. I respected that. Pretty much had to.

But about his golden years ahead, people predicted the worst.

"Since kindergarten, always our class *do*-er, Marion. Retired? He'd best stay busy. 'Cause soon as one of *those* sits down? In about a year you've got yourself a goner."

DOC, RETIRED, WAS back from Bermuda and had found his future! At our golf club bar, he spied old chums, made time to perch, tell us what he would be "majoring in" for his life's remainder.

Doc explained how, into that Bermuda resort, a decoy convention had just migrated. Dallas-based game hunters, sports-paraphernalia collectors. Too many Hemingway beards. Texas successes made high-octane boasts in an English teatime hotel.

Twenty-one days of beach can stretch out quite some distance. Doc said he'd already read the eight novels Marge brought, special. Those books just didn't seem real "lifelike," he groused to her. "Brands of cars in here I recognize but not what any of these crazy lazy people do all day. I'm bored *for* 'em."

International decoy dealers set up rusticated booths in an ocean-view ballroom. Midsummer, its cloakroom wasn't needed for men's camel hair, ladies' furs. So that space got commandeered by a covey of kingly silver-haired duck carvers flown in by private Lear.

Most decoys for sale were very old, priced accordingly. Roper, uninvited, wandering the great hall, soon asked dealers many smart young-man's questions. He proved one real quick study. People enjoy sitting beside a handsome doctor at a black-tie dinner; especially if such people have family heart histories and are over fifty-eight. Particularly if that doctor stands six-foot-two, is funny, and a Yalie still visibly in love with his very first wife.

Roper hadn't been stalking the ballroom long before organizers introduced themselves. They squired him toward the holders of the major antique decoys. Roper explained he was a virgin, at least to this. Gosh, there seemed a lot to know! The three rarest birds displayed had all been carved by one Josiah Hemphill, 1790–1842, Marshfield, Mass. Short lines formed to see those.

Doc soon learned Hemphill's big knack was a more "naturalistic" shaping, the bolder use of buttermilk paint. Hemphill had worked days as Latin master at a boys' academy. But post-declension, after refighting Caesar's wars one hill at a time, the glad ole bachelor was found paddling every Saturday and all summer with his blunderbuss and water spaniels. Hemphill, plump, gout-prone, sat amid a boatload of false ducks he carved, then floated. Wood ones lured the live ones into musket-range. You had to know how each duck species splashed down in its very own formation. Since live things naturally magnetize to copies of themselves that look super-pretty, you rope your fake-outs into just that pattern.

Buttermilk paint gave the Latin master's birds such high-gloss feathering. And three centuries upstream, their colors still looked as bright yet crackled as a Rembrandt landscape. (At the country club bar I listened hard to a subject not as personally interesting as congenital heart disease. Odd, though, it held me.)

Up close, the birds appeared no better than old paint-daubed wood. But if you squinted down, as Doc was taught, if you imagined yourself two hundred feet up, you sensed how Josiah's wide brushstrokes worked magic on the weary homesickness of passing cousin ducks. As they sought rest, their nightly berth seemed sweetened by that many family-resemblances horseshoed below.

Soon Doc was stepping onto one provided footstool; he squinted down on duck-backs laid across a ballroom carpet very very patterned.

"Aha," he said. "This Josiah's excellent, okay. Hell, he's so good I feel my *own* landing gear coming down."

Well, this crack drew lots of nods, off-colored yuks. Doc's quip would be quoted that whole Bermuda week among the real mover-shakers of Decoy World.

Over dinner, they told Roper how the Smithsonian owned six Hemphill curlews. Josiah's sole snow goose had just flown off the auction block into the Met Museum's American Wing. But Doc (self-knowledge always his R X specialty) confessed to feeling less a collector, more a hands-on type. "*Own*ing bores me, basically. *Do*ing . . . less." So his new collector-pals just walked him to the carvers.

One cloakroom had been lined with plastic sheeting to catch cedar shavings already ankle-deep and fragrant. From the look of these guys' hacked-out starter-ducks, Josiah Hemphill had long-since left the building.

Doc said he met an ex–one-star general, two forced-retirement GM veeps. Their greetings sounded jolly as their politics soon proved strictly anti-immigrant. (Spoken by a man carving a duck, the word "wetback" seems a species name.)

ONE MINT-CONDITION Hemphill—a bird that floated around in Marshfield's salty bogs not many years after our nation flew the coop of English taxation—it could set you back twenty-nine to thirty-six thousand. And that was your *bar*gain Hemphill.

Whereas a regular living guy could buy himself a pine "blank," insert a couple 10mm glass eye inserts using two-step epoxy, then shape his very own mallard for under forty bucks! "Now, that's 'a deal for real.' —Hell, let *me* try that."

Home, Doc explained to the few of us still bunched at our bar called Hole Nineteen, there are still only sixty authenticated Hemphills in captivity. "No lie?" I said, sounding false and spurned, though feeling not unengaged.

4

A FIRST FATHER-SON office visit and Roper had just fed us its complicated name. I swear he recognized our exact sickness in like two minutes. Diagnosis shushed both Dad and me. And our fair-haired boy-doctor used even this pause. He actually wrote out the name of our condition on the back of a prescription pad. He passed it to Red.

A gent, Doc guessed my dad might need to see then silently sound-out our fate one letter at a time. "Fam-il-ial hy-per-cholester-ol-emia?" My father had to hold it some distance off between weathered hands. "Let's see here. That nice little opening, the 'family' part? I do get. But the next word's being this long, looks to me, sir, like a big ole coiled black snake."

"Wish I could say you'd got that wrong, Red." Dad admired how Roper gave it to us straight. Afterward we would live in treatment. Doc's good company helped. But our Mabry bodies kept hoarding both kinds of lethal fatty juices. Doc called those "lipids." There'd been a recent horror movie at the Bijou. Called *The Day of the Triffids*, it concerned future-trees that can walk around and eat the people of the future, see. Sounded like we each had one of those growing hungry inside us. And I had taken Red to see the film.

ONCE MY FATHER made this green zone my address, I sure tried blending in. Doctors' notes excused me from gym class to the school library I soon loved. Up ahead I would qualify as in-state and entitled to our fine university. At Chapel Hill I got twenty-one A's. But it's only thanks to Red that I can *pass* today. Not coursework, either. Pass as a townie. (And surely with Doc's help in learning the ropes.)

Yes, by now I get regularly mistaken—when noticed at all—as someone born to own the third-biggest half-timbered manse set along The River Road. I've actually become the fellow wearing Saturday chinos paint-stained seemingly-on-purpose, too thrifty to throw them out, too rich to care about personal appearance while seen in a house that looks this fine. Being a six-footer of a certain silvered vintage, I appear almost natural, stretched out in a Smith & Hawken chaise longue, reading my twentieth seafaring Patrick O'Brian from our public library on this teak deck nearly seaworthy.

I greet by name our neighbors' pretty grandkids paddleboating past. I get a singsong, "Ahoy, Mister Ma-bry." Still, during one encounter in six, I expect to be challenged yet. A cringe waits half-sprung. At this age, I feel almost eager to be found out: yet another closet hick with no claim whatever to choosing hand-blocked William Morris wallpaper, upgraded to this town of nearly seven thousand!

If I still tend to hero-worship certain folks hereabouts, that habit started in my cradle. My parents spread cheesecloth over-top it, keeping off barnyard horseflies, wasps. But sometimes the white would peel away to show pure sky. Then I lay looking up at a man's auburn fringe poking out beyond his head like ropy sun rays. I kept studying a smile that couldn't help but show—in Red's own raw delight with fatherhood—his every crooked witty tooth.

GOOD THING MY folks shoehorned me into city schools early as third-grade. See, schoolmates still remember me as just one more familiar river rock, as having always lived, if hushed, among the Fallen.

Come breakfast the opening day of class, Mother asked if I really planned to wear that. See, I'd picked a favorite maroon cowboy shirt Pop had bought me at Myrtle Beach. Stitched right in were broncos, stars, plus cacti. Mom wondered aloud if I might save that back. "Maybe start out in plain black pants and your nice white church shirt? Just till we see how fancy doctors' kids dress weekdays. My way of thinking—a person can make one real loud mistake just by walking in, son. Your dad, now, he is ever a show unto himself. Short man, humongous spirits. But you and me? Though taller, we're, well, till we warm-up-like—I reckon we're more hiders." I nodded, unsnapping my whole shirtfront.

Mom squired me toward a sunlit yellow classroom. I'd dressed as plain as Mother wished. From the hallway, we peeked in at other children's sporty costly clothes. Nothing looked homemade. Soon as the last bell rang she drove our Studebaker straight downtown. Mom bought me everyone else's kind of blue Keds shoes, boys' same red-striped soccer shirts.

At age eight I still fixed my hair like the country kid I was. We then called it a "ducktail." You greased it right-good all-over, then combed not just the top but both streamlined car-detailing sides. You coiled each combful inward using a tricky wrist motion I bet I could still manage, allowed sufficient time and hair. Finally you'd give the very back a flippant up-yours turn.

Mother soon asked if I shouldn't start using less Wildroot Cream Oil. Maybe try a side part. But no, till turning fourteen, I held to my own kick-ass punk-country Future Farmers of America styling. Some Riverside girls even got around to thinking it was kind of cute! I kept smoothing my blond hair back over either ear with that Edsel-like up-swerve behind. It made me feel some kind of rural hoodlum, little Elvis come to town on market day. But my secret outlaw-pride seemed lost on the golf-crazed Fallen. Here I'd been feeling s'proud, thinking my hair made me the real stand-up reb among Riverside's club kids. No one noticed.

My sixth-grade progress note I can still quote you from memory:

> *Though Bill has kept unusually silent his first few years in a town, he cannot hide being basically kind and, certain tests show, not-unintelligent.*

"But, honey, that sounds real GOOD," Mom, my fellow hider, lifted one hand to almost pat my cheek.

I already knew their discount code for me.

OF COURSE DOC was manually skilled. For a half-century the man had always been a carver. Our Caucasian backs and fronts provided him so much practice suet. Roper's hands, three octaves wide, stretched like some Russian pianist's. He had played center for Davidson. Maybe Doc's roundball-sense in the pivot helped him see things (and patients) spatially?

Our very lack of scars, from block to Riverside block, gave surest proof of Roper's subtle digits. Everyone's beautiful glass-shattering children had been returned to them unmarred. Looking down at their youngsters' beauty, they first saw their own, then—saving—his.

In Bermuda he'd got pronounced a prodigy at seventy. Veteran carvers doubted Roper could be as new to this as he swore. Doc simply scratched the back of his fine head. Doc loved playing the rube. (Jimmy Stewart was actually a Princeton trust-funder; Will Rogers prepped at military school.) Roper lowered his eyes now, joshing, "No, I swear, fellers, this one with you tonight, it's my very first-esth . . . *duck*." Laughs.

You soon heard—through our almost-too-gossipy Riverside optometrist—how Doc had already made a normative mallard. Kind of "lifelike." Correct patchy colors, mail-ordered amber eyes, orange matte feet. Roper then elevated his subject matter to wood ducks, probably the most beautiful American waterbirds. Little stunners. You've seen them in calendar photos, their markings crisp as tux shirts. Small-sized, crested, jewel-colored. (Cooked wood ducks are said to be very "tasty." But I'd as soon eat a bald eagle or my name-sake grandson.)

We learned Doc had already developed a new paint. He was trying to copy the iridescent band of blue-green-black peculiar to wood duck males. A UPS truck twice daily crowded the narrow River Road. When Doc still doctored, working to improve us, his supplies all got delivered to his clinic on South Main. Today the delivery truck blocked half our drive (not that we were due anywhere). But what was he out there signing for, joking on a first-name basis with the boy in brown shorts?

BEHIND THE ROPERS' big split-level, a barn overlooked his three hundred feet of river frontage. Their son had used this as his ham-radio clubhouse; the girl later made it a dance-palace for teen sock hops. Now Doc was getting it remodeled into what he called his "studio." (Folks felt like "workshop" might've been a term a bit more masculine.)

The place now featured glass on three sides' cathedral river-views. Floor-to-ceiling windows 20 feet-tall got webbed across with narrow blond-maple shelving. Slots enough to hold a second lifetime's flock, whatever he seemed bent on making out there by his lonesome.

Wouldn't Doc miss Falls' charming talking-back *peo*ple? Did he not feel half-deaf off-duty without that attractive after-hours stethoscope bunched under his jacket collar? Who else had guessed Dad's and my obscure ailment in two minutes flat? We'd expected he would now go and volunteer in Darfur. *Doc Without Borders*. Roper and Marge flying off and healing the Third World. That'd prove a more suitable, fame-making Phase II. On her summer internship to Africa, a local high school girl—idealized as her age group's Marion—she had just drowned, upsetting every Riversider very much.

Doc often skinny-dipped in our river just past dawn. Nobody was awake at that hour. Except restless me, of course. I'd have taken my round of morning meds. I'd often be seated on our deck, nursing my mug of decaf (Roper's orders). As he padded barefoot bare-assed to their dock, I could see the white towel just around his shoulders. He'd plunge right in, any weather. With a nerve unknown to heart patients. I'd sit here still wearing pajamas and slippers with maybe an overcoat pulled on, winter mornings. In half-light I'd enjoy the splashing of his crawl most of a mile upriver then back, his return hardly slower than the first lap. Sometimes it seemed my doctor was exercising *for* me. And, as he stood drying beside the Lithium, seeming fully unaware of me, I did know this: if my chest seized up, assuming I could somehow make myself heard, he'd jog my way so quick.

If not exactly emotionally close in any way a fellow could quantify, at least we had proximity. For a lifetime, while he went around saving lives, I at least sold those lives their life insurance. If Doc walked through most doors into rooms that rose for their beloved, I could still slide in (out) barely noticed.

I still felt myself the ducktailed farm boy come to enter his calf into state fair competition but lacking the social skills to even go find a registrar. Doc proved the Fallens' most essential unit.

Me? a longtime voter who's served as poll watcher since age twenty-two. And I accepted our different roles. There would always be the imbalance. By now I was truly fine with it.

But ducks? Wooden wood ducks? in lieu of human lives to save? Seemed to Jan and me a step down. Inventing creatures wholesale was probably nice work if you could get it. But how entertaining? I mean, where are the surprises, your birds held together with three-inch decking screws? Chopped from cedar (soft enough to carve while staying bug-resistant)?

Still, in this second career, he must appreciate how his new patients would never beg for free drug samples. Plus there'd be no waiting for payment of their outstanding bills. Bills!

5

NAKED OR NOT, you step out onto your farmhouse porch, no one gets to see you but maybe two crows and a half-blind hog. Here? in this town of 6,803? eyes everywhere, ears pressed to phones, mouths describing your simple walk to school. Every time you stepped aside to comb your hair back nice? that'd been your Broadway audition! Each restaurant offered Mabrys, via the plain act of getting food from plate to mouth, a hundred bladed mistakes waiting. Even Falls' waiters seemed tennis line judges calling our soup-eating foul or fair.

Red insisted that we go to Chez Josephine because it was right here and, people promised, French. (Well, Belgian, really.) Brave, Red ordered, "We'll take us a load of snails, fer the table."

When those sad buttered critters arrived, Dad looked sick while winking: "You first, son. They sure look . . . educational. Let me see you eat at least one."

He enjoyed daily walks past Riverside's most beautiful homes. He invented "historic names" for his six favorites. Palladian windows sure beat his boyhood's vista, the crescent moon cut into a two-holerouthouse door. Red loved speaking with our owning-class neighbors: his concerns regarding future River Road drainage problems. "What if some freak water came surging through here, why . . ." Once home, just recounting the exchange sent him into a kind of grinning sleepiness. "Was just explaining to young Ashton, told Ashton as how . . ." This bushed look of Red's, lids half-shut, always seemed to follow his widest smiles.

My poor father's heart was so deformed, happiness cost him most.

MOST RIVERSIDE MONEY still gets siphoned from farmland surrounding us, pay dirt assumed. People admitted to fortunes made "in tobacco" but you didn't want to be caught wearing denim near a field of your stuff. If our river looks clouded brown with lithium, our land comes so packed with iron it is as red-orange as my late father's hair. Fertile crops start easterly at Falls' infamous (Fridays topless) Starlite Bar. Due west, crops edge up, then box in our Dairy Queen's parking lot. By August you eat your fast-melting ice cream out there surrounded by three green walls, beautiful shoulder-to-shoulder tobacco plants, triffids—rising silent, freakish as the National Basketball Association.

The Mabrys had forever farmed. They belonged to a dunkers' church that baptized the saved in a tributary of the sacramental Lithium itself. Yes, Red might've looked cowlicked, all but defaced by freckles. True, he appeared every inch the Hiram Hayseed. But inside there lived someone surely sleeker, paler, more refined. He'd spent his boyhood striding muddy furrows behind two mules. But his true yen always ran toward fresh-hosed sidewalks, electric-lit store windows. He praised lip-rouged marcelled town women who, as he said with some ob-gyn implications, "keep theirselves all sweet 'n nice."

Red was eager not to stay agricultural for life. He explained how persons that farm: *They are really very different from you and me.* He resented the stubborn meanness required to do battle with weevils, hookworms, floods. He explained family pride, folks being county-famous for growing one admired crop better than all others. He had competitive second cousins envied as "the Peanut Mabrys"; but he himself, as his mother never quit telling him, hailed from one uncle's branch of cousins even snobbier, "the Sweet Potato Mabrys."

6

ROPER'S BARN, NOT a barn in the sweet potato sense, started seeming a small temple-museum to whatever Doc might forge back there. We never doubted he could do something pretty doggone good. Even that miffed some on our block: it'd be hard, living within sight of a seventy-year-old model-plane-builder who suddenly constructs, say, some scale-model Cape Canaveral staging area in his own backyard. There's something Wright Brothers cranky-crazy waiting in us all. We secretly think we're always about to invent something wonderful.

But Roper's ambition was upgrading at age 70! A hormone problem? It threw into high shade even Doc's own record-71 at golf. Even I felt bitter at times, reminding myself his real name was only Marion.

And what about us? Jan and I would have enjoyed visiting, studying his modern floor-to-ceiling shelves. They were yet to be filled in like his inked Sunday crossword. Sure we respected *a man with a plan.* Isn't it odd, though? The guy was crinkled pretty old while his slick blueprints look too new.

We were over here perfecting our own off-duty slowness. Roper didn't mean to call others' bluff, of course. That would be too personal! Still, he threw into question friends' bimonthly WWII book groups, our sciatic tennis elbows, our third or maybe fourth gin(s) and tonic(s). He'd once participated. His sudden absence seemed a diagnosis.

Did he even know that my dulled hours—freed from insurance-office tedium—were partly spent flopped before any TV rerunning whatever nature show came next? What made this now seem lazy, almost simpleminded? Doc Roper's bright Phase II did.

And what, exactly, had my own Phase I been?

CAME THE DAY we could not revive my old man, long as Roper worked on that and him. Right-off Doc turned my way, promised to turn me into a Science Fair project from his days as prodigy Marion. Roper told me in advance I might expect as many as three cardiac infarctions, three spread over what time span and when. Then he told me where I'd always find him.

Doc explained just how we'd get around each one and, by God, we'd managed it so far. I say "we," and I was right there, of course. For my sake, Doc swore he would subscribe to costly cardiologic journals. He'd learn the latest blood-thinning therapies and jump-start electrode apps. Then Doc did it, he kept my chest abreast of each breakthrough in turn. And I am grateful, don't get me wrong.

But, even man-to-man, even during my final checkup in his back-office, there was still so much two fellows this full-grown just could not say. One married father of two cannot ask someone similar, *So you're taking up your artistic future, pal? Any ideas for me left couched way-back-down-in-here?*

Thank God that, early on, he'd not suggested handing me off to young Dr. Dennis S——, a too-pretty boy some called "the new Roper." Till his true criminal character poked out for all to see. Me, never trusted him. Too many eyelashes. "He's no Roper," I told one early fan. "Boy's more a stringer."

Retiring, Doc had referred me to others, though. Everybody understood that three world-class cardiologists practiced an hour and a half's drive away at Duke and UNC. Excellent technicians probably.

But, see, I didn't *know* them.

7

ON HIS RARE Saturdays-off, a certain tenant farmer's kid started hitching ten miles into Falls proper. Having discovered Riverside because one axle broke, he now went back for up-close observing. Red avoided stopping downtown. They "soaked" you, any sandwich you bought. No, for him giant houses fronting river were the real show. Red jumped out of his free ride, called thanks, simply strolled the low-cost green beauty of Riverside.

He wore what he'd worn last time: those *were* his clothes, shoes. And whose mansions were these? Owners of tobacco warehouses, furniture factories, banks, and boundless farmland, all living right along the water cheek by jowl, sailboat tied nodding to neighbor sailboats out back.

One park bench rested picturesque beside the Lithium and, seeing how it overlooked a bunch of lively funny ducks, the farm boy settled. For a good while, too. Neighbors noticed. That bench had just been placed by the Garden Club because "a seating element might look well there." It did. Red, convinced, chose to rest right here forty minutes, grinning as if about to nod or nap.

No one from Riverside ever usually actually *sat* here, really. This triangular patch of green was window dressing, first turnoff onto The River Road. It meant to say, *Gracious living starts here.* Red Mabry, thirteen, got the signal. A black Lincoln Town Car passed, then slowed to see what jewel heist this kid, rustic as a root, might be planning. Red waved.

Town planners had long ago chosen, not elms destined to die of a national disease, but durable beautiful maples. Their star-shaped leaves went from brilliant sour April-green to sweet coral-honey-yellow each fall. Even maples' bark, exposed all winter, attracted. Must resemble the smoothed sweetly-terraced backs of certain imagined Episcopal ladies hereabout.

Flanking streets, maples had managed, before World War One, to reach clear across and into one another. Now seventy feet high, they formed a continuous light-speckling tunnel.

Lunchtime! The boy Red broke out the first of two hard-boiled eggs brought as his low-cost lunch. Why pay more downtown? He knew the names of the hens that'd laid them. In his overall's bib, kept

a little blue paper-tube of Morton's salt. The delicate way he sprin-
kled it atop his half-gnawed yolk, Poppa's pinky-up gesture, why, it
would've put any snuff-pinching French nobleman to shame.

And, only after wandering around unwelcomed, after getting eyed
from various mullioned windows, after being spared police question-
ing only because he was at least technically white, my red-haired Red
hitched back to the family tenant farm.

Dairy cows stood hoofing mud, bellowing complaints. Going
unmilked hurts. Evening's warm-fisted relief was back home twenty
minutes late.

THE RIVER ROAD was Falls' single byway always crowned with its
own "The." Smith Street was nothing but a street named Smith.
But all along The River Road, owning-class folks spent weekends
wandering house-to-house holding actual martini glasses. "Yoo-hoo,
refills?" they called, entering without bothering to knock.

"I seen them do that with my own eyes," Red reported later with
one head shake. "Is that friendly er what? They flat-*know* their favorite brand of gin is in each and ever' mansion, sure as we got fresh
eggs in ours."

On our farm porch, he'd again tell us how money tends to lubri-
cate the human mind. Three or four generations into the real deep
lasting cash? Why, folks have found time to play musical instruments
and to really read. Hard books, too. "Seven-hundred-pagers!" They
learned-up about art; they soon bought genuine oil paintings, not just
for investment, no, for simple rub-up-against life-is-good beauty! Several such pictures he had glimpsed in the front hall of this one house.
And you know, each had its own electric lamp built right to the
frame? that important. Like some *place* you'd stoop and see into and
then pretty much *be* there. You could stay safe in it several seconds.

Yeah, Red insisted, the rich were—not so much "better" than
us—nope, just "different."

If we were sturdy burlap, woven to stand up under barn tem-
peratures?

They, having only lived indoors under mansion-conditions? why, they'd been silk since 1820.

8

AND WHERE WAS the man best qualified to keep me moving? He must be struggling to improve his wood carving. Doc now hid himself from view. If the man still jogged, he did it late at night. Must be swimming at the club pool, forsaking his river crawl come dawn. His "studio" light burned at all hours. UPS art supplies went in but nothing actually came out. About eleven months into his hobby, our local Arts Center invited Roper to "show."

Doc's being much missed, that likely inspired our will to see his woodcraft. Wasn't it a bit too early to show? But nobody had ever accused Roper of accepting favoritism; not this man who'd convinced us each that we were all *his* favorite.

Doc's office and practice had been taken over by one thin Brahmin Indian. We'd been picturing a small dark man with wire specs. Gandhi, really. Roper wore an actual blazer when he and Marge brought the recent med school grad for that inaugural Sunday brunch. Doc escorted Gita around our club table-to-table. He tried and make her seem truly one of us now. She had smooth manners and the right credentials and this *Masterpiece Theatre* accent. She was obviously highborn, but not in Falls. Not along The River Road.

She looked about twenty, with her giant black eyes that seemed blotters for us blondes and redheads. She wore red lipstick with one paint-chip sample of her mouth inlaid at the center of her forehead. A popular deaf old sportsman called, "Welcome aboard, young woman. You'll be seeing lots more of me. Specially during my next colorectal, Rita."

"*Gi*-ta!" Doc laughed. —You understood she'd graduated from Atlanta's Emory, and you knew that—next checkup—she'd be thoroughly prepped from your up-to-date manila folder that Doc never needed. But I later heard two gents say that, unlike with Roper, they couldn't fancy discussing with Ms. Gita Patel, MD, any of their little recent erectile issues, etc. . . .

RED GAVE HIS loved ones repeated tours of a Falls not actually his. It lay just ten miles from our farm and getting in was free . . . except for its many collection plates.

Dad admitted to a fascinated weakness for what he called "your 'town' churches." Being a contractor, he approached each sanctuary as a solemn building inspector. As the Mabrys shopped for our ideal church, bad maintenance reflected slack theology. First forays into the society of the Fallen rousted us awake many a Sabbath.

Dad's red Studebaker was always Turtle-Waxed just so. We drove to Falls to audition another neighborhood of Methodism. We were farmers entering a Protestant church that seemed barn-huge. Its pews were stocked with groomed "professionals" and our big shoes produced an echo all their own. We knew we'd never pass for visiting film stars. Sure, we understood that Falls' country club wouldn't admit us, however "country" we might look. But, not one church-usher ever body-blocked our entering even Falls' least-smiling congregation.

We surely appeared clean, our cheeks rosy from the best lye soap, our shoes spit-polished. And God knows my hair was combed! We ignored stares by doing ever more smiling. We three nodded a new-here pew-to-pew "Howdy." To make up for whatever our clothes lacked, we tried singing hymns with an extra pumping rustic spirit not always understood.

After Dad's showing us Riverside yet again, I waited for one city limits sign past the Dairy Queen. There, parents let me loosen the noose of a black tie. Most of our way home Dad offered his review of today's sanctuary and service. "Plaster around the heating intake duct in back was crumbling, see that? Deacons did a little touch-up painting but . . . And, not to nitpick, and I know it's summer vacation-time. But, I'm sorry: four people is not a choir!"

Safe again amid the quiet fields of Person County, I felt comforted. I was a Sweet Potato Mabry, native to farmland. Our ending up among the chosen frozen Fallen? I never once considered it.

I felt quite cozy enough in our tin-roofed center-hall home. A yellow school bus stopped right by the mailbox. And my dad was admired out our way. The sight of him entering any general store ("It's that 'Red' fellow, Dahlia") brought a plump wife from the storeroom, brought the yellow hounds awake.

Dad had assigned me, behind our house, a low-aerobic row of tomatoes to tend. I owned one mighty-envied cowboy shirt and, at my four-room school, I made real good grades and passed for "leader." All seemed pretty-well rooted in, nestled down. Then Red rushes through our front door, yelling. He waves around some lawyers' documents just fished from our rural box. We would get to move to Riverside. Mom and I stood holding each other. "Yes," Red said toward our silence. Yes, Mom and I, we had to come.

Colonel Paxton was, well, a Paxton. They'd been big noises around here since the sixteen hundreds. They'd donated the 1824 starter property for All Saints Episcopal plus several different golf and civic clubs, having plenty. See, the old colonel hailed from a Lord Proprietor's line. That meant his family had got its tens of thousands of acres direct off the Indians by order of some faraway English king. Worldwide chess moves broke the Paxtons' way around 1610 and pretty much ever since.

The mansion's den roof had caved from sheer stupid neglect. Paxton Hall's latest aged resident had pissed off (then stiffed) many a Falls builder. He was finally forced to start phoning contractors from outlying farm communities. Dad was barely making do, constructing housing splurges by returned GIs: an added carport, many nursery extensions. Then a revered Paxton cold-called my father. Was Red too booked? Soon as Colonel started telling how to find his home, Red's highest-pitched voice piped, "Wait one, sir. You are *not* 2233 on The River Road! *Not* that long wavy stone wall with the grass yard lately getting so full of . . . trees?"

Dad turned up to supervise a set of botched repairs. He saw at once the roofing contractor was using poorest-grade ten-year shingles, double-charging the grizzled old man. Dad confided to the colonel he was being highway-robbed by Falls' fancy-pants builders. Red offered to bring in his own country crew at half the price. "My guys, sir, are all born Primitive Baptists, and honest as the day is long, can't *not* be." Paxton, clueless and a hermit, had forever been an easy mark. He often gave that as his reason for nonpayment.

The colonel listened from an upstairs balcony as Dad fired four roofers, then Paxton Hall's most recent plumbing outfit. This struck the miser as major excitement. A certain amount of yelling happened. Paxton's huge disintegrating place was lately visited only by restaurant deliveries, census takers, matching Mormon boys.

Red soon returned to our field-view porch with sagas of Colonel Paxton's bravery in the First War. Dad admitted as how, since then, the man had maybe grown a bit eccentric. True, he owed other repairmen a fortune. But the small checks he'd written Dad, they'd cleared just fine.

Each Paxton Hall bathroom was bigger than our rental home. Each had its own huge potted palm. Each was hung with framed photos or paintings of the present heir-owner as a young soldier then an Armistice party-giver. Back then he had been as handsome as any girl can get to be beautiful. Walls around his cut black onyx tubs were paved with pictures of wild parties held here. Several such images showed the young veteran, fully bare, in all his aroused glory.

Old Paxton had lately invited an appealing young brick-mason upstairs to see what the colonel had once looked like all over. "Now, that there's . . . something, sir. Mighty frisky you got to have been, sir. Yeah, well, better get back to work, outside and all . . ."

Paxton spent much time soaking in a faceted black tub, one located upstairs, one down. There he received carpenters and Chez Josephine takeout while, goatish, reading the New York papers. Each tub looked big enough to seat four. Hard to believe what poor care he'd taken of that God-given face and figure, not to mention his inn-sized house. But Dad swore that the old gentleman still had, hidden under all his gingery growling, an absolute heart of gold.

Neighbors complained about his lawn's weeds till those became the saplings now a tangled forest. If you didn't know that one stone Georgian house sat jammed back in there, you assumed his yard must be the start of a state park. Dad had begun bringing his newest boss man jars of Mom's famous pimento cheese. The old colonel felt amazed to have finally found an employee who'd return to the job-site weekends without charging overtime. (Underbilling could make you into a local whispered myth. True, both Roper and Dad did it. But, for me, poor as we started out, it's something I have never cottoned to.)

Paxton was glad that at least one visitor proved brave enough to risk death ascending the free-hanging spiral staircase. Creaking, it'd rocked there half-moored since Falls' wildest party ever. Dad felt honored to be received at any home along The River Road, especially one with a name famous locally since 1610. "Red, you're overdoing," Mother warned as always. See, my father had taken to performing little private repairs off-book for free at Colonel Paxton's. The blustery owner, wearing striped pajamas, would get right down on the floor beside Red, handing him the wrenches and coping saws Dad was forbidden to use.

I visited Paxton Hall just once. Dad promised I'd enjoy the old man's tales of killing certain Huns hand-to-hand. I was nearly eight and the old guy up past eighty. He looked me over and announced, "Lucky features, considering." Dad laughed. "You mean he favors *her*? Yeah, averaged out good. The Lord was merciful in that at least. And Colonel, the boy's smart as he is pretty, though he'll blush, my just saying *that* . . . See, what'd I tell you?"

I remember Paxton wore a long maroon bathrobe (silk, I guess) and two-toned golf shoes and that was all. His shins showed cuts and bruises I now connect with stumbling alcoholics forever at odds with the world but, first getting outdoors to that, battling their own furniture.

He talked about certain local ladies he had experienced, naming names, imitating sounds they made during. He edited no sex-misdeed for a child's sake and I bit my lip for shame, preventing further coloration of my whole face.

But as the colonel sat there, his robe untied and he revealed a nasty lack of underpants. This confirmed my worst suspicions about old old families, old and increasingly careless. Given wealth enough, certain tribes, like certain people, experience wholesale second childhoods. And, with the Paxtons, thirds.

In a year or so, Red had sold timber rights to the mansion's frontyard, then got it tamed enough to mow. Its U-shaped drive wore new flagstones. Pop got the house looking at least half as splendid as it had during certain hunt balls of the Calvin Coolidge years. One Saturday, almost a year into their curious friendship, Red turned up uninvited, carrying a potted geranium; he'd brought some of Mother's excellent banana pudding the colonel now swore by. Steep front doors stood open. Red soon hollered from chamber to chamber, checking bathrooms first. He found a naked Paxton floating in the upstairs tub beneath that day's sogged *New York Times*. Turned out the old pennypincher had left my father sixty-five thousand dollars and his founders' legacy country club membership. In 1955, 65 thousand seemed to us, and others, one mighty pile of cash.

Paxton's kin lived widely scattered. Most sane people, with *that* kind of money, depart Falls first thing. They'd had no news from this family grouch in decades. Two California nephews threatened to sue. Who ever heard of a handyman inheriting so big a settlement? But, arriving at the improved mansion, finding it habitable, despite old neighbors' horror tales, Paxton's nephews piped down. In the end they let one little miracle-working contractor keep his nest egg. Hell, hadn't he earned each cent? Imagine nodding through their shell-shocked horndog uncle's latest tale of one brilliant Verdun trench maneuver leading—as if underground—to a particular bawdy post-war Charleston pool party!

Dad at once made down payment on a cottage just big enough

for us but with a River Road address. It was not, he admitted, at the best end, "Still, it'll be our foot in their door." Mom and I stared at each other, purest dread.

9

JANET, NEVER ONE to wait, got my attention that first week among the Fallen. I sat enduring third-grade, feeling too new here, wearing unfamiliar Keds that pinched in back. I just occupied my desk, staring shamefaced no place. Today's topic was the Panama Canal. I felt somebody look directly at me from the left. I glanced up and over and there she sat in rubber-banded pigtails, nearest the window, staring.

My eyebrows lifted to ask, "Well, *what?*" But she simply nodded back. She did this as old farmers nod to other fellows their age— strangers met by chance downtown. Fellow sufferers. I found I could meet her gaze, could true-enough hold it. I looked away but guessed I hadn't really needed to. So I glanced again, just checking. And since that second, little has changed in her being there—wry, curious, direct—always able to respond, unblinking.

And on day one, age eight, she did something odd. She placed one index finger to her lips, forming the *Shhh* of secrecy. Next, this Riverside banker's daughter pointed my way while indicating some crook-fingered angle. She seemed hinting I should look into my lap. Foolish, I did so. Zipper fully down, pouched jockey shorts showing like opening day of the Panama Canal. I closed my eyes but did fumble, did manage to fasten things, without another soul's noticing.

When finally I found nerve to scan her way again, that girl sat focused only on a very distant Panama and our real local teacher. Hmnnn.

BEFORE THINGS CHANGED, Falls felt like a waterside retreat from foreign riots, congressional morals that'd coarsened. It was particularly sweet for those of us adults holding a certain amount (and kind) of money. After sadness hit us hard, you started hearing charges against longtime elitism.

The River Lithium's current encouraged for short stretches white kids' sailboats. It busied the bamboo fishing poles along the water-front of "Baby Africa." That neighborhood's name lived on from just after slave days. It had been proudly picked by freed black settlers. More recently, sensitized Riverside liberals like Jan and me, we've gingerly abbreviated Baby Africa to *B.A.*—Like *L.A.*, or like short-hand for a baccalaureate degree. For decades Jan and I had daily fetched and returned from there. We were transporting our coconspirator, Lottie Clemens. She's the long-suffering woman who helped us rear our Jill and Billy, helped keep our home decent. B.A. also provided all the caddies and wait-staff for our Broken Heart Country Club.

—Disaster makes you doubt every decent thing that stretched back safe before it. Till then, I swear, Falls mostly kept busy amusing the *rest* of Falls. Each according to the jokes and styles of his-her own neighborhoods, naturally. Our town sat isolated amid square miles of growing tobacco. Out this far from the next village, we gave our kids piano lessons because Sunday afternoons we still wanted to hear our children really play. We *had* to entertain, inspire, and, where possible, worship one another. Who else?

And it was in this loyal spirit—only when we turned up en masse to support Doc's "art" show—that we saw how pretty good he'd started getting. Everyone was there. The Bixby twins lunged in, half-grown, hair slicked back and always looking like they'd swum in, sleek dark boys. They stayed understandable fans of Doc. Though they were named Timothy and Thomas, our town had changed this thanks to pure musical affection. "Where are *Tim*othy and *Tom*othy?" people had slipped and said from the start, and it stuck. That was how we greeted them today.

Gita waited just inside the door. Even her sunflower-yellow sari could not upstage our beloved ole bone-saw. There were just eleven

wooden birds displayed. They floated in mirrored glass cases fitted
with clear shelves so's you could see how, even underneath, Doc
had got each one's proper little rubberized feet tucked up golden
underneath.

That these blocks looked just like ducks was a given. Doc, in
everything, never fell below a certain level of finish. But past that,
these seemed separate spatial puzzles, perfectly solved, each completed, elegant as algebra. Is Authority something native to certain
hands? Where do you either learn or—likely failing that—buy it?

Our *Herald-Traveler* (atypically accurate) mentioned in its next
week's issue:

> Doc Roper has shown another side to admire.
> He caught the personality of certain ducks.
> Here a joker, there a beautiful young mother,
> next "some bachelor drake on the make."
> Marion Roper offers his viewers more than
> Field and Stream craftsmanship. Though ana-
> tomical care is surely evidenced. Our ex-
> doctor's finest work gives us, you might say,
> duck-portraits. Who knows, folks? These could
> even be "featherier" versions of our much-
> missed GP's beloved familiar patients.

And we, at the Falls Arts Center, buzzed on the good Napa champagne that Doc must've subsidized, stood around . . . feeling glad for
him, if a little landlocked. "Familiar patients"? heck yes. —"Beloved"?
Given who Roper was, that would always be harder to prove.

We were . . . not *jeal*ous of the skill exactly, just made a tad
jumpy by it. (Folks untrained in art tended to call one carving
"good" and the duck beside it "really super-good.") Admirers grilled
Roper—had it not been hard to actually begin again? A whole new
field, or stream? Must be. The start right when you turn seventy, are
you kidding?

Art lovers asked Roper: How much previous experience had Doc sneaked in, carving? Hadn't our Marion cheated, getting so good so fast?

"As to my 'practicing,' before? I'll tell you, friends," Doc confided, scratching the back of his white head. "Marge always made me carve her a whole turkey . . . most Thanksgivings."

Diana de Pres, still our greatest beauty despite ugly jagged life-time binges, cozied up against one whole side of him. Janet rolled her eyes at me as our beauty insisted, "Immortalize me. Do one of *me*, top to bottom, Doc!"

"You wanting a portrait-carving or your final physical, Diana?"

Hoots of laughter. This is the kind of cornball line that everybody loves and re-quotes in our sidelined self-amusing Falls. Pathetic what we sometimes settle for.

I O

I WAS EIGHT when, the Paxton legacy deposited, Red shifted our church affiliation accordingly. He transferred membership from Second Methodist clear up to First Presbyterian. "Growth pains already," Mom said under a sigh pancake-sized. For years we'd com-muted Sundays, ping-ponging between denominations. I'd once called it "stained-glass window-shopping" and Dad acted as pleased with my term as Mother found it troubling. Red immediately asked me which church window, in all of Falls, I'd like best to wake up looking at. I answered, "The rose window at First Presby. Because . . . if God was candy? that's just how He'd look."

My father slowed the car. "This boy . . . I swear, this boy will, no telling, this boy . . ." Dad bragged to our Lord and to his rearview mirror.

His standards for church music also remained very high. He felt that Second Presbyterian's able choir stopped itself just short of becoming loud or overly-melodic. Their plain white sanctuary seemed both a kind of IOU to the next world and a tasteful apology for this one. See, Red Mabry was edging us ever closer to full-blown watered-silk Episcopalianism. I think he believed that the air in All Saints' stained-glass sanctuary must be so rarefied—with its incense, 1820 German pipe organ, founder-families' names spelled out in wine-dark stained-glass—that, simply on entering, all our country noses would bleed.

But, arrived to live along The River Road, Red finally started admitting certain long-held snobberies. Against some new neighbors. Dad confessed he just didn't respect, not next-to-nothing, Riverside's tobacco bosses. Cigs were even then called "coffin nails" and got instinctively dodged by anyone with tickers weak as ours.

But furniture manufacturers? Now, those Dad rightly admired: "A chair is something you can *point* to."

And he mentioned a big Queen Anne townhome that had been fully funded by one family's brewing-distributing nonrevenue moonshine during Prohibition. "Still, it's the same type-a-money as these up-and-coming Kennedys'." Red did yield a bit. He had the absolute standards of the absolutely powerless. But how he enjoyed them.

TOO VISIBLE AMONG the Fallen he embarrassed Mom and me with his color-blindness. He stood enameling our sweet Cape Cod cottage's front door and its every shutter a tomato-red high-gloss. "I'm sorry," Dad stood back, squinting. "But, that? Now, that there is *class.*" Grinning, still countrified as salt-cured ham, he'd pronounced the word, "clice."

Mom later guessed that, with people forever calling him "Red," he maybe over-favored that shade? The color looked mighty bold in a neighborhood that still considered forest green a wee bit racy. Then Dad went and named our simple house. He awarded it a historic distinction somewhat at odds with its being a Cape Cod two-bedroom thirty years old.

"Shadowlawn" was the title he invented during one dreamy weekend spent striding around our half-furnished home in his boxer shorts. He kept muttering words that bore no relation to each other, except in his surging visions of family crests, his hope of finding one drop of blue blood among our hearty, if thinned, red.

"Glade . . . Rock . . . no, Cliff . . . Scarlett . . . Castle . . . something. 'Fern-leaf.' Nope, I reckon a Fern IS a Leaf, mainly." Mother and I tried not laughing. But he remained in a trance like some bright ten-year-old girl the day she discovers Poetry and runs around quoting reams of it at her older brothers then finally the canary.

Red next commissioned a sign. It would rest, explanatory, on our extremely unhistoric lawn. First he had woodworkers strip a pine log of its bark. Then he ordered the word SHADOWLAWN carved in relief big and deep. Letters' fronts were paint-rolled lipstick-red to match our cottage trim. The final product looked like something you'd see for sale at a roadside stand near the Everglades.

This item did not stay on-duty long.

WITH MOTHER'S BLESSING, with her actual bribe of a soda-shop trip for me and my new steady girl, Miss Janet Beckham, I sneaked out front after midnight. I yanked Red's sign from our newly-seeded yard. The marker had scarcely lasted halfway through its first duty-night, explaining us. Overexplaining us to a Riverside already too amused at our lottery-like arrival. Into one docile river, I heaved the non-word *Shadowlawn*. Lettering upward, cheerful as a duck, the log did not sink but happily bobbed elsewhere as if seeking finer property to describe.

By breakfast Dad found the thing missing and, boy, was there Hell to pay! Red pressed short hands over his face going redder. "Don't let me get wound up here. You know what Doc says. They come like a thief in the night. More jealous out-of-towners! Thrill-seeking souvenir-hunters. Low. And I bet you anything, by now it's up over their damn mantel. If the poor devils even *have* one! I always do say I just hate when criminal-type-a-vandals can't help a-preying on such gentle homes as ourn. But still, you know? At least they're history-minded. Looked at one way, why, it's a *compli*-ment!"

I SAT UNDER a terrace umbrella at the club alongside Janet, my demure teen date. She wore a sort of sailor shirt, pigtails unified now in a single brown braid clear down her back. This would be one of our earliest public outings and Mom had made the reservation. Jan and I, too young to drive yet, had walked here, a shorter hike than going clear downtown. We decided, like bohemians, to have dessert for lunch. When, thrilled, I told Mom this, she said, "Go ahead. Don't guess it'll kill you."

Waiting for our treat, I found I had too little ready conversation. But with so many classmates in common, I pictured walking from desk to desk for topics. And I had just started a not-too-fascinating alphabetical roll call. "I see where Bobby Blanchard knocked his front-tooth out skating . . ." When we both overheard a high-pitched country voice from just inside. Red, not knowing we were here, had arrived at lunch to meet his afternoon foursome. Janet and I, pretending to act unparented and if possible Parisian, we just drank more from water glasses. We soon endured having to hear Dad. He got introduced to a bank manager new to Falls. "Welcome, welcome." Pop sounded like anything but a quite-recent newcomer. First, Red determined where exactly along the social-tape-measure of The River Road this fellow lived. "Aha," he said. Then, satisfied, Dad asked his usual tie-breaker.

"I guess you-all's new doctor has got to be Roper, right?" The stranger explained that, being so new here, he hadn't needed medical help quite yet; but folks did say that it quickly narrowed down to a choice between Roper and this young . . . Dennis, was it?

"Let me save you a peck of trouble, fella. You seem like a nice man. It's not no contest to it. See, my family, we've always just thought the absolute world of Roper. Why, when he takes you on he takes you on. And Doc, see—it's a long story—but he is doing . . . Well, he's flat keeping me and my precious boy alive, is all."

Silence fell at about seven tables. Ours had been hushed all along.

I myself went very still, my top lip feeling numb. Janet claimed to have been listening all this while to a woman across the terrace. Seems the gal had recently accused her ex-best-friend of being a kleptomaniac, see. Of having stolen one entire bathroom scale from this first lady's home during Bridge and then carrying it off in a huge handbag brought-special. Took it right next door where anyone could see that missing scale on display in the guest bath beside her *first* one. I faked interest but saw Janet was protecting me. She did that. I'm still not sure why. She swore she found me nice-looking and way smarter than I credited myself. Who could not be grateful?

This had been about my first try at it: taking a girl out on something planned. And it'd been going just excellent, too. Then we had to sit upwind of my old man, with Red blasting our private news to one and all. You think I wanted my girl to know how sick I was?

Though our banana splits arrived, I could not quite enter in. Before lifting the cherry off-top hers, before enjoying that at once, Jan touched the back of my hand. Said just, "Every family's embarrassing, Bill. —Now look what-all we have here. These walnuts, you think?" and lifted her long spoon.

Why had it felt so shaming? To hear poor Dad promote our Roper tie? And for some total Yankee stranger. *Why* was his testimonial this painful, Red's country overtrust? For one thing, I decided, eating, it'd sounded like some sharecropper's loyalty to his contracted landowner. That seemed not quite manly. More a slave's allegiance. Sounded kind of clingy and reminded me of something, but what? something very unpleasant.

Oh, yes, this: My father had just said out loud, before fifty people, exactly what his quiet son too often thought when safe in his own silence.

"Kept alive" by Roper? Well, no. But yes.

Still, who needs to hear that while you're out in public and with such a nice girl?

MY FAMILY'S BEING new to town, with neighbors peeking through venetian blinds, with me in need of buddies, us Mabrys mostly kept to ourselves. Farm-trained, we were used to it.

Humoring Red, Mother stayed more mindful of his heart than he could bear to be. Some nights Dad swore that all those doctors, even a wizard like Roper, had been flat-wrong. Accusing him of heart disease? Hell, that was just their way of keeping a good man down. But, even as he said so, you could hear he didn't believe it. The very tiredness making him complain was itself our diagnosis. I listened hard, already knowing that his fate was mine. Surely my folks had meant well; but I wish they'd not explained my heart disease to me my very first day of county school.

Dad had inherited this weakness from his sharecropper father. That young man, William R. Mabry the First, also worked as a tenant farmer despite his constitution's failings. While pitching hay he was known to black out, topple right over. His loving wife, always on guard for him, rushed forward to tell other hirelings, "Just leave him be. My Will, he'll get his wind back. Just do what I do. Work around him. Oh, he'll spring up." One day Will did not.

Some people receive birthright property. My chances had been fifty-fifty and I'd lost. From my warmhearted dad I had drawn a lipid-squirreling impulse that no known antidote could lower. Before we found Roper, less good doctors had spoken of our condition only by its hurtful initials. They called what we had "Coronary Artery Disease." Then they cruelly shortened even that to "C.A.D."

WE WERE SHAKY if grateful the day Doc Roper straight-out admitted our poor chances. Country doctors' summations had usually run: "You two? Got you two bad hearts, is what you got. You should *hear* yours! What to *do*? Well, sirs, slow down some. The second it gets to hurting you, I mean right when you feel 'full' across in-here, well, there's your sign to rein in that particular activity. Oh, you'll get the hang of it. Just can't do everything. It's pretty much going to be like this. —Anything else?"

Roper instantly had the name and numbers; it made me know that a grand education is one that leads you to specifics fastest. He stated how some people simply cannot "process" cholesterol, good or bad. The body holds all of it. Soon that same flawed body begins to farm its own stashed lipids out to its extremities. Lipids will soon coat the linings of basic plumbing. Then they'll clog the free-flow that living requires. "A slight genetic twitch," passed from father to son, leads to numbness in the hands and feet, to living tired then fully-winded, early endings guaranteed. Roper admitted right off: this meant that my own son, if Janet and I had one up ahead, he'd get the same fifty percent chance of being a carrier. I loved Doc's honesty but feared he told the truth. That meant, while still a relatively young man, I already lived around the crusty pump of some guy pretty-old.

There's a kind of wisdom that comes from this; but, me, I am still seeking that. I keep holding out for some factory rebate. Maybe I was destined to sell health, fire, life, property, and flood protection to Riverside's most prosperous and therefore fully fearful?

Red sat asking, "Doc sir, since you've told us what we got exactly, is there still no drug for it? What has science even been *think*ing about?"

"No perfect solution yet, Red. If I were you two, I'd pop niacin pills about like chewing M&M's. There's a new product called MER/29 but I don't like the side effect in pigs and rabbits. Cataracts, size of grapes. Those'd spoil your developing golf game for sure. —No, your boys' ticket is regular exercise. But avoid Olympic trials, Red, got me? One study was done on folks with rheumatoid arthritis—seeing if aspirin could help their terrible pain. Didn't, but cut their incidence of stroke and heart attacks by more than half. Sounds crude, but it's cheap. There's no literature yet. So don't be telling anybody I urged an aspirin a day on you, all right? They'll think me some quack. Cigarettes? even being near others', deadly. Oh, and Red, I saw you having your way with the club's fried chicken. That's out now, hear? You'll want more greens. Since both your bodies retain superfluous lipids and won't relinquish even . . ."

Roper noted Dad's frown. An eighth-grade dropout's dread of excess vocabulary. Like magic, Doc's RX shifted, "See, Red? Is like this: Your body, when it comes to this fat? it's all Savings and no Checking. So, we've just got to work at cutting down what's being taken in. Your body can't stop chucking every bit it finds right into Savings. Your cholesterol-account's so overloaded it's started clogging your heart. And, sad, our young Bill's here."

I felt Dad, seated beside me on our shared exam table, nod; I almost heard Red's heart-click of recognition. He'd finally understood in plainest terms our bodies' strange and killing greed. Roper saw: only his simplest explanation had eased us both.

And with us, father and son, still feeling uneasy even at being bare-chested (if only before Doc), with us each feeling scared of a curse that'd leave at least one of us alone and soon, Dad and I did allow it to happen just this once. We let my bare left shoulder touch Red's right, then stay massed there, to warm it.

I knew that Red would face his own incoming death with some forward motion of belief, acceptance. Time came, he'd rush clear out to meet it. He'd try converting it into some awaited friend.

I sat here, shivery. Sat wondering—just as we held one disease in common—might I someday match him? I mean in pure simple spirit.

Just then, to be honest, that seemed unlikely. And my fear of cowardice around our illness meant I'd earned myself a disease far worse than Dad's.

I I

TURNED OUT LATER, Bobbitt's Hobby Shop downtown had been underwriting Doc's exhibits. Why? The week his first show opened,

shop business (according to "Bobo" Bobbitt) jumped 39%. Doc's golfing chums lined up to learn any "art." Even a few on-sale woman-craft
macramé outfits got sold in plain wrappers. One well-known former
Wake Forest linebacker bought a whole "Dolly Village" to take home
and paint. The huge man asked, "Bobo, can I put snow on their roofs?
'Cause I like it when there's snow piled on their little roofs."

Being only regular people, these fellows carried home ready-made
"kits." Roper'd assembled his à la carte. He'd gathered the best tools,
first in Bermuda then via contact with other duck-nuts on what he
loved to wink was truly these guys' "World Wide Webbing."

"Doc definitely got that computer out of its crate," I told my wife.

MUST'VE BEEN AROUND then, Janet read to me from *Parade* magazine how a writer said way back, "There are no second acts in
American life." (Wasn't my Red the exception? We guessed Roper
hadn't heard yet, either.) Doc still talked about the upcoming joys
of a man's middle-age. Imagine pretending that seventy-one was
your Big Game's halftime. Life span 142 years? Sounded reason-
able for him.

You started seeing his name in more newspapers than our *Falls
Herald-Traveler*. Even the Raleigh one. He still looked handsome in
his leathery laugh-lined way, hair a purer baby-powder-white. His
smart chuckle could sound half-mean, and always that textured bari-
tone my wife called his secret weapon. Odd, his kids now spent even
their Christmases skiing Aspen or hitting the books at far-off Yankee
grad schools. With Marge still looking thin and dark and pretty
darned "good," the Ropers seemed to be taking Excellence to some
new high-water mark. They looked . . . well, national. Something a
bit disloyal there.

"Oh, face it, he's always been a little bit of a secret show-off. Admit
it," Janet snapped my way one morning. I sat washing down, with
decaf, all anticoagulants he'd long ago prescribed. I knew she meant
well but her roundhousing on Doc just made me feel worse. He'd
done okay by me, and even by Dad at the end. Whenever a good
doctor retires, his patients must feel a little jilted.

Was about then, us locals began collecting decoys. Coincidence? We all did live along a river, too. Whatever made us notice decoys, they soon became our minor craze hereabouts.

Mallards, gadwalls, pintails, redheads. Real duck names sounded so funny and like toys, you'd want one of each.

FADS REQUIRE DISCRETIONARY funds. And I guess Riverside had right deep pockets. Old farm-owning families had arrived in town to join the Fallen just after Sherman smoke-cured our county's grander homes.

By now our own friends' kids were marrying, several per weekend, another sort of biologic fad. Our lovely daughter's wedding I'd nearly paid off. She is so gifted a linguist, Middlebury tried to hire Jill her senior year there. If I start to boasting, I'll never stop. Our age group retired early. Youngish lawyers with serious golf and rogue drinking hobbies showed a growing willingness to spend weekends cohabiting under and alongside hangovers.

Certain made-up customs we enjoyed. Les Wilkins had spent much of his tobacco fortune on collecting antique cars. He'd filled an old family auction-house downtown and hired two black men to mind the fleet, keep it all tuned up. Every few months Les would drive another one up The River Road, taking kids for rides, pretending to try and pick up his friends' wives. "Judy, you could have had me in this. Instead you chose to be with Ted who is now-bald? Say, Ted still got that trusty '96 Taurus, does he?"

Les was no stranger to bourbon but somehow Tennessee-Kentucky's by-products always cheered him. He owned one grand limo that'd belonged to Gloria Swanson, a giant gleaming thing, all wicker panels and silver running boards. And, right before Christmas, after sufficient eggnog, Les would throw a wreath over its hood ornament; he'd ease along slow, honking its old-fashioned trumpet horn that, for some reason, played the first eight notes of "I'm Forever Blowing Bubbles." If we got near Christmas and hadn't heard it coming down the road, we noticed, even fretted. These are the amusements of those of us who stayed. Everything becomes our own

Fallen advent calendar. And in every window, one colorful local. Personalities, the clock chimes you could count on.

Televised sports showed games local fellows used to play a bit less well than they remembered. We still loved the way our houses looked. As outlying mallside suburbs filled with crude copies of Riverside Colonials from the 1920s, our originals, themselves rushed copies, looked taller, more "historical." But even our Lithium's recreational waters bring us the stray unpleasantness.

One evening Jan and I were cooking outdoors for our bunch from the club. Somebody looked off the deck and upstream past Roper's studio, and wisecracked, "Think we've got a country guest. Who invited him, Bill?" It was a dead white Brahmin bull, floating. Thing was massive, pretty swollen-up, far-gone, and its male gear on show was either huge or distended. The beast had a set of long hooked horns; the end of one had somehow got its curve jammed into the crack of one rock. Over the mossy stone, water steadily flowed, shifting the poor creature's front hooves as in some dance or seizure. Sure looked like he wanted to get loose. The bull appeared as tired of being seen as being dead.

Jan gave me a stare that said, *Take charge for once?* Though I felt willing to put on hip waders, crank up my never-fail Evinrude, prod the beast loose with one oar, I instead suggested we move our nice picnic indoors for a change, what say?

Next morning, merciful, he was gone. Then, scanning downstream, seeing no trace for a clear half-mile, I felt concern. Almost missed him.

12

YOUNG BLACK CADDIES at the club quietly instructed Red. At his invitation they kept offering Dad small hints at how he might seem more at ease here. Though Red was a legacy member, these new pals hinted he might quit using the establishment's full name.

Shorthand is one perk of membership. So Red abbreviated his usual, "Shall we meet then before our one o'clock tee-off at the clubhouse in the Nineteenth Hole Bar of the Broken Heart Country Club of Falls, then?"

The Ice Age gave our club its name and odd emblem. On the cusp of one hillock rare hereabouts, nature once deposited a perfect igloo-sized stone. Seven feet tall, five wide, resting on its side, it was a giant accidental replica of the standard Valentine heart. Its twinned halves looked smoothed and rounded as buttocks at their best. Formed by chance, the thing must have busted in transit, maybe being pulled along what we now call the Lithium. Though elephant-gray outside, its inside surface showed a shiny jet-black all geode-angles. Long before Columbus, something split this thing into being a landmark the Tuscarora had navigated by. And since the 1600s, settlers had all called it the Broken Heart. You saw it inked in shorthand on our earliest English maps.

Since then, many a risk-attracted teenager, including me and Janet, had smoked around the thing, puffing, squatting. Disavowing our country club parents' hypocrisies and shallowness, we kids avoided rain by hunkering under its valved halves. We crouched for shelter near the gray sides like its own pink piglets. A broken heart so big seemed to call forth our rare tourists and the Fallen's many lonely kids. The ground around our namesake Broken Heart was mulched with generations' cigarette butts.

When Colonel Paxton's parents donated eleven hundred acres to become the course in 1901, once their family refused to let our club be named for them, this great boulder seemed the natural next-best. For locals, "the Broken Heart" referred mainly to this familiar geologic feature. Only out-of-towners ever thought the name odd for a carefree sporting institution.

My wife's sophisticated visiting college roommate Kaye sometimes ate with us there. She once asked, looking around our club's 1920s raftered stuccoed dining room, "So. Are the broken-hearted the ones turned down? or you people actually paying dues for this?"

INHERITING THE PAXTONS' founders' membership for free, Red chose to purchase used golf clubs. Why? He told Mom and me he dreaded other fellows guessing he'd never played before. "Chances are they'll *know*, sugar," Mother allowed herself the smallest of her cat smiles.

"Oh. You mean when I try and hit it and all, they'll guess?"

"Maybe you should first practice, in the backyard . . . of *Shadowlawn*?"

"Genius!" He admitted, "It's just that our move up and ever'thing, well, it's happened so danged fast. To be listed among the Fallen and then in Riverside to boot! And now, with 'club' this, 'caddy' that. Sometimes being in town full-time, I hit certain aspecks and just don't know how to 'do'!"

Mom again warned him not to strain himself. In those years everyone still walked the course. With Red become a daily club regular, I—trying to fit in at grammar school then junior high—withered, picturing him.

I'd been drafted into the ranks of the Fallen and had not volunteered. I tried keeping some of my country stillness. Jokester chatterboxes forever need new victim-listeners, right? My thoughts? Oh, they run fluent enough all day as you can hear, I hope, I hope. Only parties, just living groups of four or more, still tongue-tie me. At gatherings, me early, folks entered, smiled, called my name, nodded, speed-walked to the bar.

But Red? Red sometimes sported too-new tartan golf caps ordered from catalogues. One had *Saint Andrews* stitched across its bill. He'd never been abroad, he'd clearly never played the mythic course. Surely others, knowing this, would spare him, not asking him to reminisce. I, hushed as ever but wide awake, found my father's overstatements grueling. Right on cue for being fifteen.

Red embarrassed Mom and me only when we caught him somewhat fudging. If Dad stayed just what he was—what all Mabrys were—he was hard not to love. I just ached to see him make wishes so blamed visible. But, for him, putting them out there's what made them real. Hadn't this already brought us sixty five thousand and a house in town? Me, I felt eager to help him learn to hide. Was I best at keeping my own dreams secret? or had I not yet fixed on one?

Red kept slinging around those overused clubs. Kept dropping Roper's name as if a school chum's. Dad loved the Broken Heart so much he even praised their so-so chicken lunches. He believed the wives of his new dentist-friends all looked like certain movie stars. "Hiya, 'Rhonda Fleming.' You do, too. Just LIKE her." He made himself pathetic, upbeat and therefore indispensable.

Guessing he'd never be taken for a full-fledged Skull and Bones member, Dad gradually became—without quite knowing—a sort of rustic mascot. Most smooth Falls golfers had secret kinsmen hidden one or two counties away. Their uncle-farmers looked and sounded not unlike my dear clay-colored Red. So gents—by shaking hands with this new member, by accepting his very presence as the last of weird Paxton's many pranks—felt slightly better about *their* secret country kin. Executives now decided they could tithe at Broken Heart. Now their own sun-cooked uncles and forty male cousins need never set a muddied boot onto the black-white-checkered marble foyer of an actual Riverside home.

Black caddies gathered around Dad, grinning at his jokes regarding bulls and cows, town salesmen outsmarted by farm gals. Red wanted to know young caddies' plans for some eventual education, better positions in out of the rain. Certain club members could always be counted on to slip bag-carriers a few bills and the same funny remarks. They often asked about the young men's getting lucky on Saturday night, how lucky and what was her name? all that night's names? Ha. Red seemed innocent of any difference between the Paxtons and their hired repairmen bag-boys. Since before George Washington, Paxtons always had the jobs to give, right? And poorer fellows needed work. Poor boys had been honestly paid to smooth things over, mop up after each smart-mouthed Paxton since 1610. Fair exchange of services. No shame in that.

I once overheard a golfer fondly quip, "Well, you know what ole Red says . . ." I also heard Dad called "Yosemite Sam, over there." Times he made me want to either blend in fast or fade away completely. Having arrived among the Fallen without heightened expectations or faked confidence, I mostly kept to myself. Poor health reinforced that. "No roughhousing ever," they'd told me on the way to first grade. So I tried to look tempered, naturalized. If a high school fad for madras pants broke out, I made sure to be among the *last* to buy my pair. Mom resembled me in this. We kept tucked-back safe.

One Sunday Dad was driving us to First Presbyterian when Mom announced she'd reaffiliated Baptist. Her chosen church looked like our old country one. We'd liked it okay before Red's craze for all things "town" landed us on Lithium's shores.

Mom found some perfectly nice women at Third Baptist of Falls. They worked as seamstresses and kindergarten teachers. And when they drove in to have tea with her, one admitted to writing down the River Road address beforehand, in case police stopped her, she could prove she'd been invited.

I made friends too, quietly priding myself on talent-scouting the best folks, not the flashiest. (Doc was the only "famous" fellow I ever really cared for.) It so happens that some of the finer people on earth are forever—arms-crossed, shrewd observers—waiting there, off to one side. Always at the jury-box edge of things, silent for a thousand reasons of their own. Mom and I found few saints strewn among the Fallen. But those pals would, like my fact-loving face-saving Janet, prove lifelong.

THOUGH RED WAS freed from farming, though he knew local stores didn't open till nine a.m., he rose early and hit the shower. He counted on its metal stall to improve and echo his Tin Pan chorale. "High as an e-le-phant's eye!" became my reveille. Mom and I stayed bathers, hiders, silent afternoon soakers, readers in the tub. Honestly, if it had been left to us, all Mabrys would yet sit fly-swatting

on some hot rental porch midfield. We three would still be right
out there rocking tonight, comforted by roosting chickens' late-day
placement squabbling, studying someone else's tobacco acreage. Such
land's main beauty was the horizon where—for our inexpensive sidelined entertainment—an entire sun set nightly.

Even groaning during Dad's wake-up serenades, I'd come to
half-appreciate his nerve. I, as the town boy who borrowed a record
number of public library books, soon realized how much room
there is on earth for one true believer. My very gift for camouflage
let me see Dad plainer. Every club and lodge and church needs at
least one Red Mabry. One who'll make only positive remarks, one
who always offers unfaked enthusiasm. Raw belief. In the value of
believing. In what? What have you got? My father, a pure person,
put forth nothing else but faith.

Dad could hardly bear to even drive us past All Saints Episcopal,
1824, slate-roofed, ivy-wrapped, Tudored with half-timbering. He
knew the Black Forest town where its organ had been made, given in
honor of Colonel Paxton's kinsman, killed in the Spanish-American
war. Jan and I once caught Red sitting in his car nearby on a summer
Friday night when their organist always practiced. Passing the place,
he'd sometimes whisper, "Inside, too, it must look just-like just-like
being in England."

I've never known anyone with less education and grander fantasies.
It made you marvel at his potential. It made me forgive his granting
me this lifetime-break called Riverside. Your ticket to the middle
class is, once punched, irrevocable. If you can truly taste the difference between a four-dollar supermarket Chablis and a true reserve
Malbec, then you have tasted of the apple, or the grape. No return
trips. Heaven and Hell do not accept each other's currency.

Times, I wonder what sort of country Buster Keaton I'd have
been, if simply left out yonder hoe-in-hand.

Times, I still feel like some well-fed wild creature mistaken for a
domestic pet.

13

SOMEBODY SUBSCRIBED TO the top collector-carver magazines, then passed these along our riverside road mailbox to mailbox. We soon learned those Hemphills were called "gunning decoys," meaning the kind once built to really float. But such game-trapping had worked too well. By 1912, all that got outlawed for commercial use. Decoys had become so good at teasing migrations down into killing range, whole species were going extinct.

Only then did the craft of outdoor trickery become the art of mantel-worthy carving. Our dear America itself, such an excellent invention, first ran Westerly and wild. Then all that reversed too-soon; it galloped on back and right into the Chicago stockyards.

America, how soon you pulled shut barn-doors behind you!

Even before WWI, we'd changed over—from being a nation of hunters to growers, from outdoor do-ers to collectors of the former do-ers' nifty gear. How weirdly soon we came indoors!

One side effect of being told since childhood that your heart's diseased, you pay steady attention to breathing, to any available banister. Over much direct sun can seem a threat; you get to imagine your own death scene. It's a privilege—mapping-practice for your final voyage. (Red Mabry would get just the communal public death he wanted. Other loving men stood by in sweet attendance.) —Would mine, my death, occur on some ab-improving machine of Broken Heart's weight room? In my car after activating the turn signal then pulling over, ready?

It can be an advantage, knowing. You must prepare, admit. But in most directions it's a hideous deal, getting your death sentence so rottenly-early. Age six. And yet *when*—not *if*—it comes, I'll grab whatever poetry that last free throw can give.

ROPER NEVER SEEMED to age. It wasn't only I that thought so. He'd been years ahead of me at Falls High. But our class still bobbed in his choppy wake. His dad was known to be the handsome sulker, nursing a drink at bar's end, always a silk hanky in his blazer pocket, forever the pack of new playing cards ready at hand. He proved as addicted to contract bridge as he was awful at practical finance. But, however dapper a business failure, Roper Senior had not *bought* prestige for his son. Unlike so many of these D+ jerks in presidential power lately, Doc simply made up his own credentials. He won scholarships that were, as they say now, "need-based." Everyone in Falls inherited a little something. But all Doc got from his parents was their poise, their length, their pianist's and cardsharp's tapering blond hands.

In a town so small, we rarely speak straight-out of "love." We go with "think the world of him." But didn't we share one river city's circulatory system? Small pond, one truly big duck. Big Doc.

Something in his approach felt both eager-beaver Boy-Scout-like and yet still "cool." "Doc always goes all-*out*," our conservative crowd said, with admiration and worry. We fretted how his too-public enthusiasms left the man exposed. (Not that *he* bothered noticing.) Unlike most of the Fallen—company-men with cousinly ties to R. J. Reynolds—he lived with no sponsoring endorsement. Doc didn't teach at a university hospital, too long a commute. As our general practitioner, he just generally practice, practice, practiced.

Everywhere you went in driving-distance you somehow heard of a new oddball syndrome that Doc alone had diagnosed. Once at a country store outside Castalia, the clerk asked where I was from, then told me how a man named Roper, visiting this same spot for fishing bait, had found the clerk's young niece going into a convulsion never seen before. The scared clerk guessed it must be sudden epilepsy till Doc discovered, wadded in the girl's locked fist, a wrapper from a candy bar with peanuts. "Here's our problem. Bring me—let's see here—your Dristan powders and all your pills for poison ivy."

Protective, we felt scared for Doc, or so we told ourselves. Thing was, he still expected far too much. Might not Roper pay, and big time, up ahead? Or must we?

When he bought his first white Volvo wagon, the Falls Car Dealers' Association held an emergency breakfast meeting. The GM boys admitted to the peddlers of new-here Swedish and German and Japanese imports, this was one mighty dark day for all things U.S.-made. "What's bad for GM is bad, man."

And sure enough, within a year, twelve other admired young Riverside couples defected to Scandinavia, then even switched over to our two recent enemies at world war.

The Cadillac dealer afterward admitted, "We should've kept the Ropers supplied, free. Course, he's way too proud to just accept a fully-loaded El Dorado, boys. We might shoulda rolled one into his garage, gassed, waxed and ready! —Our *de*coy, get it?"

NO FALLS COLLECTOR could yet spring for a real Josiah Hemphill. But seven homes already claimed their signature "Marions." Oddly enough, he'd dropped his lifetime "Doc." Man went back to that aunt-ish ferny ole first name. He incised that moniker alone beneath the tail of every creation. That followed by a needless ©. —His nom de plume(!) contained no hint he'd ever been a Yale MD. —Now, you delete a fact like that from your CV? means that, for America and Falls, you really are already sailing in your own Phase II.

TRIAL-DRUG TESTS, early transplant lists, Doc pulled all the strings he held to keep his promise to me current. Roper hoped to get gangly me and this weak-fish heart over the fence into *my* Phase II. He always blamed himself for not reaching my own dad in time to save him. No one could have. My own final office visit with Roper, he had taken a prescription pad and jotted three names plus their switchboard phone-numbers. "Who's all this?" I asked.

"Best cardiologists at Duke and UNC. The Sultan of Brunei? he had his triple-bypass done at Duke. They say he rented the university hotel's top three stories. For his wives, kids, security and rugs. Travels with his rugs. They're his capital. He'd obviously pick the best heart guy alive. —So, Bill, what with me being at this age, I guess today means the torch is passed."

"Making me the torch, huh? Go out pretty easy, torches. —But thanks. You more than tried." And into my shirt pocket I double-folded strangers. Seemed kind of "cold" of him, but what had I expected? He couldn't stay on-duty for the sake of one. Not even for his next-door neighbor, truest pal and leading advocate-observer.

Though I was a serious case, Doc never charged me one cent more per office visit than he did certain hypochondriac ladies. They had highly seasonal complaints. Friends said with a laugh, "With spring coming on, he'll soon be seeing Julia, I bet. Julia usually gets all her 'lumps' in April. And so, poor Doc takes *his*."

(And yet he never shamed her.) "Well, Julia Abernethy, you still look great, and I think you're a perfect saint to bear all you do, dear gal!")

Looking back, how had he abided us these forty years?

14

ONLY ON ARRIVING in Falls did Red understand he was exactly as short and yam-colored as folks had always said. A "Sweet Potato Mabry" after all, he drove downtown to buy his inaugural seersucker suit. He learned at once Falls' best "good" store. All the Broken Heart golfers wore this store's seersucker, striped brown or blue, the one suit suitable for your summer church or lawn party needs. But Rosenblooms' veteran salesmen always made you face three mirrors. You could see the whole back of your head and it felt almost sickening, a dizzying double-cross. Poor Red came home shaken, acting seasick, went straight to bed. Now he knew he'd forever live eighteen holes away from clubhouse handsome.

At supper, hair uncombed past caring, Dad said, "Praise the Lord, you don't favor *me*, son. Good you got your daddy's fixtures but your momma's features."

Mom was basically pretty. But her pale rounded looks never seemed to give her either pride or pleasure. "Everybody's got to look like *some*thing." Baptist-again, she turned aside our every compliment.

Tonight Red kept at it. "Boy, if God had to go give you my bad heart *in*side, thank God ole God at least let you be pretty as your momma in the *face*."

I blindly accepted Dad's belief in my looks. Though, like Mom, I never trusted that I appeared like much past *occupant*.

Once at the club shower room, hiding on the shy side of my opened locker door, I had to overhear some guy say, "Yeah, wife got us there so early, only people around were the caterers and Bill Mabry. Oh she apologized then!"

I OWN A coveted Evinrude outboard, mine since youth and therefore now antique. Its green metal sheathing had all gone to crumbly rust. And yet the thing turns over every time, humming stupidly forward. Doc once joked about buying it from me. "Won't quit. Like a certain nearby rusty aorta. Your ole inboard, right, pal?" It relaxed a person, having as a heart one barnacled if stubborn combustion engine.

Maybe half of healing means passing another week's false confidence to the gimp? If so, bring me even more. And I can say I loved the man for giving my own slowing life at least this image.

SOMETIMES I WANTED Falls to change and then it would, but rarely quite the way I'd hoped. When Jan and I longed aloud for "new blood" it came, but bringing traffic, people that did not know us, or even Doc!

If big money once flowed from farm shacks to riverside town houses, the circulatory system reversed. Former fields, having given up tobacco, now sprouted malls that leached residents and cash from downtown. Jan asked if I'd drive her to our one good dry cleaner on Main. Though we'd last been here a month before, everything somehow looked unpainted and old-fashioned.

Along Old Town's Summit Avenue, our founders' mansions seemed swollen, stairways dangerous for families with kids. The best such, home realtors had gussied up as new insurance firms or B&Bs. A historic marker before one rambling house explained our last Confederate soldier had died here in 1940 (attended by his funny over-worked nurse-wife). The place now served as a law office. Its big front yard sign declared NO FAULT DIVORCES, CHEAP. IN AND OUT.

I remembered riding into Falls with Mom and Red for window-shopping. The sidewalks were both washed and swept. We would step solemn from store window to window. The lights were brilliant. The clothing dummies looked to be New Yorkers. And we stared in as if hoping to join their church, too!

That same downtown lately looked smudged. It looked unloved and therefore unfamiliar.

MY HEART ITSELF I hoped might just maintain. I saw no high-jump meets in my future. But my inboard's chugging did let me perk along and notice our deck's river view. I focused more on my wife's recent sighs around three p.m. I fretted over our kids' uneven early career advancements. I concentrated on keeping our house painted, always harder so near water. And on our beloved neighbors, the Ropers especially.

He told me at our mailboxes how one wooden fowl might take him one month to three to craft. That meant Doc was not the speed demon he'd always seemed. Such carving was exacting but his paint-ing, he admitted, took far longer. My Janet marveled at his "color-sense" she called it. "Most men can't pick out more than basic red or white or blue. But these feathers he does, they're more an olive-green shading toward the weak yellow from our cockatiels' backs. I read somewhere, color-blindness mostly happens to men. Who knew he had this *in* him?" But we looked at each other and knew we'd known. He could've run the Mayo Clinic blindfolded. Compared to that, what was an excellent custom duck-coating? I heard he owned a couple brushes inset with just three camel hairs.

After his second exhibit, even our least arty guys in the younger set began to talk up decoys. What *were* these except hunks of wood with flashing cuff-link eyeballs? During drink-hour, people passed around their original heirloom Marion—hand to hand, some weird scrimmage. This pintail's surface felt sanded into soap-stone, jade. To the touch, it seemed less plant matter, more some cool mineral. You almost needed a magnifying glass to appreciate the many quills he'd scratched in there; no single feather assumed. His eye on the sparrow. Each quill built, as by some architect, atop* the one beneath it. "Good as new, pal," Roper used to tell our son, after suturing his eyebrow shut again.

And, where did lucky owners keep their Marions? Not in safe-deposit vaults but out atop their coffee table's magazines. Our con-tinent's wildlife had been tamed to hold down a job now, mere paperweight. Had all our native wildness shrunk to a decorator accent securing our now-married daughters' back-issue *Vanity Fairs*? I finally admitted it to myself. I wanted one. I wanted one he'd made.

TWO NEIGHBORS NOW hunted decoys on eBay. Fellows were soon ordering any thirty-dollar hunk of speckled cork and beak. They would bag no Hemphill, no Marion that way. All of us on The River Road now knew just enough about aquatic-bird-carving to make us dangerous, snobby. (Since Doc had never let me pay him his true worth for necessary Monday office visits, I imagined I might finally off-load major cash, buying one main "art duck" dead-ahead.)

I don't want to make like the Fallens' only news came via fake birds, Jack Daniel's, and our kids' early publications. We had the usual vigorous adultery and dicey legacy-mental-health. Money woes, plentiful heart disease, overmuch ovarian and breast and prostate cancer. Usual. Locals dependent on tobacco money were sometimes driven—out of defensive product loyalty—to smoke. They'd prove the act harmless. So tobacconists and their young kids publicly stuck with it, always good for a free pack, jaunty with the cigs as FDR in profile. They stuck with it till cultivating group lung-cancers they could've surely lived without.

And one night Les Wilkins's dad's bankrupt tobacco warehouses downtown caught fire. (Luckily spared, the old auction floor where Les stashed his priceless car collection.) From our decks in Riverside, the whole downtown looked outlined in flame. Silhouetted church steeples made this seem a godly retribution.

Farm-communities were glad to feel needed by the Fallen and rushed us their every truck. The whole night yowled sirens. It felt like London's Blitz, great cascades of upward sparks hung red against stars' cold blue. But what came drifting upriver across Baby Africa then into Riverside? This smell so fine it seemed almost an idea! Tobacco-dust, all of it that'd ever sifted into floorboards or rafters since Sherman's worst, lit up the night like one fine trick cigar.

If tobacco tasted as good as it sometimes smells many more would be dead. And this seemed history's long final exhale. Jan and I soon shifted our deck chairs to face such hellish fireworks; we waved over at the Ropers, ditto out on theirs. Studying orange sky, we breathed a luxury that can only come from the very last of something. Even our superb vintage poison!

Clowning, Doc leaned at a deck-rail, himself pretending to smoke, blowing great sophisticated rings of nothing. Then, seeming to remember, he pointed over at me, tapped his wristwatch, signaled toward our house.

Just as my Janet here had first mimed news of my raw zipper, Roper stood showing—in a gesture coded for me—I should stay out, enjoy this exquisite smoke briefly, but soon head indoors, okay? Too much of it would not be good for me. Eye to eye with him, I nodded. And all this understood between semaphoring buddies sixty feet apart!

Things had a way of circling back around among us, like our shared S-shaped river. Two couples who'd noisily divorced married opposites—"change partners," as in square-dance geometry. That and the humiliating arrest of a longtime Riverside klepto were good for about two years' talk. We'd lately dodged four hurricanes. One friend's grandson, 8, died in five weeks, of unlikely Rocky Mountain spotted fever. (People said Doc, unlike Gita, would have recognized it right away.) Two pals got hit by lightning on the Broken Heart course standing under the biggest maple just as they tell you not to. And one local scandal had state police staking out a nearby nature-

park men's room. It'd become the "meeting place" for a certain type
of highly-sexed lumberjack.

It shocked us when the culprits' familiar names got listed unfil-
tered in our *Falls Herald-Traveler.* The shop teacher with a cleft palate,
our own bank-trust-officer, one beloved black choir director father
of six. Firings resulted, yellow moving vans arrived and departed. A
town less colorful.

The cops had used their youngest blondest cadet to be bait. *His*
name went unnoted. A competition sprang up to learn if he lived
among us. Shocking to hear a deaf old pal at our club say too loud,
"I'll give fifty bucks to any man can tell me the name of their Decoy
Dick."

BEING MYSELF THE largely self-taught son of an eighth-grade dropout, I can now let myself feel briefly smug: about our three curly
grandchildren with IQs bound to produce cute stories. "Bettern
money in the bank," I know my dad would enthuse.

One five-year-old grandson (William Mabry IV) recently explained
to me by phone, "Kindergarten? Boring, Grandpa Bill. Always the
same. Milk, cookies, cookies, milk. But, know what? I'm breaking up
my day more, see. Time goes faster when I try and teach the others
fractions."

As a kid, you start off feeling different from everybody else. But as
time keeps washing you along, you grow half-proud of how animal-
alike we are. Whoever escapes that? Who'd want to?

Here I could, but won't, mention professional high points of my
son (Haverford, Stanford) and daughter (Middlebury, Baylor). But, at
my present age, the town itself seems a fraternal order I'm proudest
of. Since I'd stayed here, Falls naturally stays central in me. This age,
I set less store by my particular role in this madhouse beehive. We're
all in it together. The law of averages throws us some geniuses, some
psychos. But one stabilizing force shepherds us in-betweens, us souls
born to stay local.

In the end so much comfort rises from our river. Whenever I get jangled, I just step out onto our deck. I'll inhale whatever lithium haunts the mists. I note today's water level crossing our six flat giant rocks: I listen to what today's major note is. Often a G. I swear this little river's become my nitro and my prayer.

Out here, I ask myself if Red did not die a disappointed man; moving Heaven and Hell just to get us into Falls, only to find his son an insurance peddler. But why beat myself up? I did my best with those cards palmed my way. And now? I've retired for exactly this purpose: to meditate not medicate.

We often eat lunch at this table Jan keeps draped in oilcloth. She says the maple's droppings stain her better inherited linen. Sitting here I at times imagine this same musical tone after me, post-Bill. Like that rock ballad about life's "running on within me and without me." Will always be. Our standing houses still looking beautiful for our genius grandkids.

Sometimes I wonder if people's final seconds alive do bring that fabled highlight-reel. The life-flashes-before-your-eyes-type thing? Hope so.

That in itself must feel like an accomplishment.

15

IN MY EARLY twenties, I got dibs on Roper's first Monday office slot 6:45 a.m. I held it too, even skimping on vacations certain years. I'd leave Janet at the beach with Lottie and our two, after driving them to Wrightsville the Thursday before. But my Mondays were essential. Doc's nurses treated me to my own coffee mug, filling it, black; even as Roper warned again that I should skip caffeine. "Then how will I *know* I'm alive?" I said the same thing almost weekly. But by now it'd become liturgy.

"Well, Bill." He shook his head to one side. "You've got a hard choice ahead, looks like: quitting either the excitement of coffee or . . . Janet."

"One lump or two?" (My stabs at Doc's dry humor never quite made sense but we laughed anyway.) Bad health was good for at least one Monday cackle, a quick visit regarding something irrevocable. In sickness and more sickness. It ran on like this for decades, our ritual. And, between us—to me at least—it all seemed, life and death, charged up, so *per*sonal.

Before his long hands cupped the stethoscope to my front then back then front again, Roper would huff across its stainless steel (which clouded at once). His spare heat weekly took the edge off a natural chill. And soon, me seated bared to the waist, he standing fully-dressed in whites, we'd just be catching up. Between certain needed vital-signs-listening silences, Doc was quick to offer the mild neighborhood lore I loved.

Me, I never could gather much on my own. I've heard far less since he quit us.

Stated like this, our lifelong office visits sound routine. But, maybe their coming at a week's start and just past dawn, maybe that let every visit seem an extension of yesterday's All Saints eight a.m. service. A Sabbath-annex gave my week's one basic warrantee—his genius tinkering on me. He kept making little shifts in my meds. Placebos, busywork maybe. "Better, worse?" he'd start some mornings.

And what could I offer in exchange? I had little past my job-slot, insurance, group life. I had my goodwill, toward him at least. I'd gladly shared my father with him, right? For that he thanked me with my life. Doc seemed at one with all he did. With none of the levels of qualms and exemption I seemed to always bring. Roper'd just scribble out the new prescription, more as subject matter than any real cause for hope. Then he'd pat me on the bare back, also a sign for me to get dressed; he'd send me forth: "Steady and holding, pal. I'm liking the sound of the ole Evinrude inboard this week."

I mean, it meant something, you know?

THE ARTICLE IN our latest AARP bulletin was titled "At Last Un-mortgaged, Second-Chance Lives Newly Afloat." Big as life, there Doc and Margie were on record, page 96, photographed in his retrofitted Riverside studio. White interior walls surrounded his workstation, a world mostly glass. The Swedish-modern shelves showed—in curly-tailed profile—his past four years of daily work. Quote:

"I do try keeping my best ones held back for myself," a lean Roper admitted. "I find I like being around them daily. My quorum. As with family, you hope to learn from living close-by your finest early mistakes!"

Bet that made his absentee kids real happy.

STILL, YOU WERE mainly glad for him as yet. Maybe it was one use for his intuition. But, if your hands contain the power of life, wouldn't it seem a demotion, to have all that wasted on wood? Sure, wood lasts. But to what end?

And yet, I figured, even now, with him retired, even with his taxi meter set to "off-duty," if worse came to worst, my Janet could always run find him. And if she had to interrupt close-focus bird-carving? I wouldn't mind.

Magazines spoke of his being belatedly "discovered." But hadn't we known Roper all these decades now? Even so, must be wonderful for him. I'd chanced to see his studio light burning, lately past three a.m. Of course Doc's art must've been some true form of *work*. But somehow, to me, it felt like slacking. Roper, as usual, seemed to have gotten away with everything.

Invited to exhibit new birds at the British Decoy and Wildfowl Carving Championships, he and Marge got flown to London. Only during his third local show did I see how much he'd grown. Imagine, older than I and still getting daily better at something! A display case off to one side was labeled MY LITTLE EXPERIMENTS. —Pretentious?

This material seemed far more private than his finished projects. You felt you got to scan some Nobel scientist's lab notebooks. Onto wooden wings and tail feathers, Roper kept trying to shape believable water beads, see.

If you borrowed Janet's 3.0 bifocals and bent close, you'd note convincing pearls of water. He had coaxed these up from the same hardwood that'd formed the feathers damp beneath them. Doc then saturated the droplet with a glowing sheeny gray-blue. We heard he'd figured out this paint formula in his see-through studio no home-towner ever got to visit. Parked across its lot now, we now noticed high-end Lexuses (turquoise) with New Mexico tags. You saw the yellow Hummers of photographers from big-time magazines.

Folks made corny local jokes about how "people living in glass houses shouldn't stow loons." There he kept the best of his best and we learned he'd had a killer burglar-alarm installed. You knew why—once you stooped before this glass case, once you studied Rop-er's carved water. You almost wanted to break through glass yourself. You'd risk the cuts. If only you could touch the outfanned wing and its spray of river water.

Wet would probably come off between your thumb and forefin-ger. Odd, but this liquid seemed legally our community's. Didn't it truly hail from our local river? And, though you knew the big drop-let was just wood, gesso, silver metallic paint, it'd surely feel oily with Doc's essence, some luxury hard-earned, it'd come off slick between your fingers, pure native DNA.

16

SINCE GRADE SCHOOL I carried in my back jean pocket (1) the all-important comb, and (2) a doctor's excuse: "Bill here must take Study Hall not Phys. Ed." True, the note bought me many happy library hours. It also forced a kid to imagine the circumstances of his death. All before he's quite plotted out his life. True for Dad, too.

But he'd long ago adjusted. Even as an honorary town person he rose before first light. Showering with off-key show tunes, he was like the rooster who thinks his rusty song alone orders the sun into place. Though Dad no longer needed to work hard, he kept taking odd jobs. "For fun," Red shrugged. He admitted with a droopy half smile, it was also one way of getting into those giant homes where we'd not otherwise be welcomed.

To repair such piles, he hired the few Falls plumber-electricians he'd judged trustworthy. Dad stayed loyal to his country crew but their trucks seldom seemed operational; that made their even getting to town strangely hard. Red guessed the Primitive Baptists felt uneasy among the fourteen-inch crown moldings and orgy photos of the Fallen.

Dad had helped Doc Roper build his own home dock. Dad could walk from our place to this split-level Frank Lloyd Wright knockoff being remodeled. Marge Roper said, "We were told it's based on Fallingwater." But the Lithium ran outside their house not through it.

Doc and Red had taken to each other at once. Roper was just then opening his practice here. He and Marge had bought the big river place. It was a financial stretch for young marrieds but I guess that, like Jan, Marge had some old-family money. Rumors varied quite how much. Starting out in practice then, Doc still traded his services for others'. He'd accepted one man's lifetime house-painting in exchange for family office visits. I wonder now if my father didn't do Doc's jobber-overseeing as a swap for more frequent family cardiac checkups.

Red's specific case (and mine) seemed to at once engage our young GP as a scientist. This disease, passed from father to son, was just beginning to get some of the research Dad and I felt sure it deserved. Not long after I moved back home as a graduate of Chapel Hill, Roper invited Dad and me in for our joint monthly consultation.

Only then did I finally ask Roper how he'd been so quick to recognize our obscure condition. He pointed to Red's eyelids. Flecked skin under either brow had always been slightly alligatored. Doc explained these pocket-bumps were stored cholesterol. The body couldn't deploy its horded lipids fast enough. So the organism stashed such gunk at outer edges only. Mabry bodies were laboring to keep at least hearts' arteries clear.

"In worst cases, you'll see a circle of cholesterol rising up from within the eyeball itself, a perfect ridge around the iris. But on that count? you both look free and clear. Eyes good as new."

After a final pressing of his warmed stethoscope to our fronts-

backs, Doc stood directly before my shirtless father, "Say your own
dad died young, Red? Remind me, what age exactly?"

"Well, sir, let me see here. He'd of been right at thirty-six, yeah.
Sure was."

"And, just beforehand? had he been particularly stressed? I mean,
what was your dad *do*ing when he died?"

"*Stressed?* Daddy was plowing. It was '34."

"Aha. Makes sense. —Well, I don't want either of you going anywhere near a mule, hear? Even if a nice one keeps bringing its bit and
harness up to you. That clear, guys?"

Dressing, shy, we thanked Roper. He'd given our problem complete attention. I searched his face and manner for just how dire it
was, our disease. Did he admire us less now? Still, we Mabrys sure
felt singled out. Later, I'd worry that Doc treated everyone this way.
Of course I knew that was a merit. Should be. Even so . . .

"OUR" DOCTOR, ROPER forever put my dad at ease in ways Red
rarely guessed were planned. Roper combined the strangest quality of being both an ordinary-sounding guy and our truest local
aristocrat. Some saving coolness always pressed right up against his
warmed front surface. Some short-term joke hid his long-range plan
for you.

Maybe old Paxton had enjoyed the actual pedigree stretching
back before this wilderness got itself up as a republic. And Colonel
Paxton might've finally become a true philanthropist by rewarding
my father's innocent faith in beauty and a good address. But, it was
Roper's calm that eased our country tribe into feeling half-secure with
its strange new life. Doc's own gambling father, his mother musical
with sighs, they'd at least taught him the sort of manners that never
seem just manners. He let the Mabrys' being healthy appear someday possible. Roper made even our sudden club membership feel, if
sudden, somewhat natural. Was this just part of his doctoring? Or
did he truly mean it? Or was it maybe likely some of both?

I WAS FRESH home from our excellent state university (nation's oldest, chartered 1789). Red had wanted me to join some fraternity or at least get into a fine new dorm. I found myself happiest renting in the small mill village beyond the university train tracks. There I noted a FOR RENT sign hand-lettered on a worker's whitewashed cottage. It seemed brother to the one Paxton had sprung us from.

Janet attended the Women's College in Greensboro and some weekends I'd hitchhike the fifty miles to her campus. She was studying art history and her student art show painting (of the Lithium) won Honorable Mention. It was not abstract but I thought it was the best. Thumb out, headed toward her, I always felt a little wild, and closer to my dad.

UNC professors knew nothing of The River Road. Its codes and demands would sound laughable to such Harvard, Princeton men. "Parochial" was their own fond word for this beautiful state that underpaid them.

I worked hard there, wonderfully anonymous by choice. Teachers soon seemed to respect my mind, even some of my writing. I got to study Homer, a bit of Latin, European history alongside advanced math. I came home to find myself both over- and underqualified. Finally I turned up a temp job at Riverside's best insurance agency. The boss needed a salesman Boy Friday with a club membership, someone from our water's-edge neighborhood. I guess I was the only Riverside college grad adrift enough to consider taking such a position. Sure I belonged to Broken Heart, but I stood to inherit little more than my father's name and house.

The insurance mogul was a golfing bachelor and, after six months of my being punctual and somber and concerned, he told me he sure liked my clear blank style. "But I have to say you give new meaning, Bill, to the words 'silent partner.' Still, I prob'ly talk enough for four, and your sales're solid. People trust you. Widows especially. Some guys just have that. Can't be bought." Two years later he said he'd someday pass the firm along to me. If, that is, I didn't find such work too painfully dull. He'd long ago confessed: His well-paid secretary ran all the triplicate paperwork. Adjustors working for our national firm assessed the actual damage. I would sell people on protecting their lives and property. How hard could it be?

The boss managed to stay out most days glad-handing new clients on the links of Broken Heart. He was obliged to drink with others after hitting around a few balls, all a write-off and a lark.

At his office Roper explained to Dad and me how, given our disease, insurance would prove a great choice for my talents. It'd prolong my life. "If dealing with people's crazy made-up claims doesn't leave you barking-mad. But deskwork, that's the ticket, Bill. Let people come to you. You have a face they'll like then start to count on. Just don't go climbing rooflines like your mountain-goat poppa here. Oh, I saw you up checking slates on the Blanchards' roof. —But Red, I'm like you, hate sitting. Far as that, here's my latest advice for you: Quit your playing all eighteen holes. Nine's plenty. And, for now, just once a week, hear? Clock more time on that putting green. You need it almost as bad as me. Oh, I've seen those big swings of yours windmilling up and down the fairway. With that much upper-body work, Arnold Palmer, you might be taking risks."

"I do put ever'thing into it, Doc, sir."

"Yeah, I see that. And there's your trouble, pal. You heard of 'heart trouble'? Well, steer clear of giving *your* grade of slippage a bit more trouble than what it's got. So let me slip you one last tip, Mabry Senior . . . Hell-for-leather as you're working those links, don't hire any of our young hotshot caddies. They're in such an almighty rush to wedge in one more round a day. Just make you anxious, their advice. No, you'll want to ask for old Maitland Miller. You've seen him, tall, white-haired fellow, keeps to himself? Tell Mait I sent you. He's been out there since that course was still fine Paxton tobacco. Mait, now, he's older than you by 'round twenty years. He's not going to rush you. Be good medicine, letting him pace you. But, even better, Red, I'm told there's great sport in contract bridge, one mighty fun game . . ." And you could see Doc bank a smile. He knew he'd set Dad off and now leaned back to enjoy it.

17

JANET AND I had known Doc and Marge since forever. But despite my feeling free to see Doc at his office pretty much anytime, invitations to the Marion Ropers' home became less forthcoming. We had all been young marrieds together. Then we'd enjoyed two full seasons of their direct social grace. Who knows why they'd taken us up, then set us down again?

Was it something I said? Did I agree with Doc too soon? Or stare at him too long as he stood showing how he made his potent unbruised James Bond martinis? Maybe I forgot to thank Marge as I was leaving once?

"We were too close already, living right here," Janet shrugged. "Those two can't turn over in bed without our hearing." I gave her a look. "Well, you know what I mean."

But it felt painful. With them so busy and so near us on the river. It's not like they threw massive parties and cut us out. But we couldn't help noting which three couples the Ropers preferred this year (ones way younger than us, of course). And every five to seven weeks, here those beauties all came, carrying champagne and flowers, hollering indoors ridiculous new nicknames. We ourselves felt equally "attractive," "up-to-date." Jan and I read certain articles in the library's *New York Review*; we'd forever subscribed to *two* newsweeklies. But I reckon old friends like us are often the last to know. Was it my sickness? Was it our son's being Haverford and his at Harvard? He could have told me. I would've accepted it.

And yet we still loyally waved to him reading on his brand-new redwood deck. "It's too red," Janet said (to please me).

"Oh, honey, it'll fade soon enough," I called, as if taking Doc's part, only not.

Then Roper would be out there shirtless, strapped into bandolier binoculars; he'd become a crazed birder.

Not two years ago, this guy had been considered one crack duck hunter. His office watercolors had shown dawn-silhouetted boaters, guns aimed at chevrons of doomed incoming geese. Now, he acted grateful only for those bagged birds pals brought from the coast. These were handed over for Doc to study. Roper had gone passive-pacifist thanks to retirement and to art. He now stored his specimen-waterfowl in a huge Kenmore freezer bought just to keep these fresh. We heard how Doc had given away his excellent inherited Browning (to their help's rambunctious teenage sons!). People said he lived almost as a vegetarian, so reverent had he become after daily meditating on his flying-swimming creatures.

He stopped making certain pointed jokes. He then stopped "getting" them. When a beloved cutup shoe clerk saw Doc step into his store, the owner called, for all to hear, "Please waddle into our web-footed section, Donald Doc." Roper gave him one scalding look, veered out. It'd been a stupid thing to say but was meant as tribute. To survive in Falls, you have to take a joke. Or pretend to.

Neighbors judged our Roper had floated a bit above his raising. True, his bridge-obsessed dad had "class" if rarely a spare twenty. — And now Doc was letting any cut-rate airline's magazine come photograph that precious studio, while never admitting his closest Falls admirers.

Still, I owed him.

It was at his third show I saw it. And chose to buy his all-time greatest work of art.

18

NOT TO BOAST but, from twelve feet's distance, I spied Doc's masterpiece. Roper's *portraits* of wood ducks were, I'd admitted from the start, unbelievable.

In the wild, wood ducks are, of course, the prettiest things you'll see dressing up any American creek. White specks, red beak, eyes almost lime-green, really God's own Woolworth paintbox. A chestnut-colored breast spread with white dots the size of daily aspirin. And this one had a jaunty crest that looked back-combed just so. A little Elvis, not yet drugged unhappy, but already a tad aware of his own damp swiveling beauty.

I bent eye to eye with this plucky bird. I met myself, age fourteen. Even the bird's swept-back "Mohawk" somehow spoke to me. Now, how to *adopt*—meaning *buy*—this punk of a duck. The thing, first glance, just had such *heart*.

Prices were not posted. I saw none of the usual rash of red stickers meaning *sold*. I felt embarrassed offering a close friend many thousands for something of no use, except your looking at it. Which is a use, I guess I know.

Even so, really really wanting it, asking for and getting Janet's own nod, I finally cornered my pal. "You signed the bottom of this bird, Doc. Now let me show you I can carve my name at least across the bottom of this check. Jan and I will give our little guy a nice dry home. I'll take him."

Such a smile Doc gave me. "Bill? Gosh, I'm honored. Truly. Fact is, seems the way this world of decoy collecting is set up, I'm expected to park this particular baby with a top Manhattan collector. That way, they tell me, Woody here will be seen by certain museum folks. Don't ask *me*. Seems that's how ye ole art world flowchart works. But there'll be others ahead for you and Janet, promise. You've got quite an eye. Wood ducks give me the biggest headaches. So they're always the most fun, like my best patients, you regulars, m' best patients. I hate that a New Yorker's already called dibs on this little dandy. But nowadays I'm putting all my new things in the agent's lap first-thing. Easier, finally. —But I sure appreciate that interest, Bill."

"Aha," I said. I stood here. The checkbook in my hand truly felt like my dick hanging out for all to see.

I stood remembering his cruel joke about my son's clumsiness, even as our boy lay there gray-green with a bone-jutting fracture. "Well, Doc, thanks for even con*sid*ering our offer." Politeness kills the fastest. "*Real*-ly. Just to even be considered in the running . . ."

He sure heard my edge. He knew my heart. He'd once described it as likely someday "to flutter then, quite honestly, implode." Doc now stepped a full foot closer. He even clamped a hand around my bicep. I tensed it quick into a bulk more manly. Roper hinted under his breath how not even HE could pay retail for his own darned carvings lately!

That too hurt my feelings . . . I guess I can afford what I usually set my heart on, thank you very much.

Fact is, not to talk ugly about him, but Roper was becoming kind of "artistic." I don't enjoy stating this. But it's sure what others were saying. Suede elbow patches appeared overnight on the old blond tweed jacket locals had seen on him since Davidson. He and Marge had bought a young pair of Josiah Hemphill–like springer spaniels, though everybody knew he'd given away his dad's one beautiful unhocked bird gun. Janet predicted worse, "When we see him smoking a Sherlock Holmes pipe, we won't be too shocked, now, will we, Bill?" How could I even tell Jan about his turning down my offer like this? Still smarts.

(In North Carolina, we've always put a premium on modesty. Mom advised I was already a lifelong "hider." Still, it's wrong to let others guess you have real money. Best underdress. No cowboy shirts inside the city limits. Understate to the power of five. That's code here. But even so, I would have paid him twenty-five thousand for the damn thing is all I'm saying. Thirty. No, I'd go clear to . . . sixty-five. —I mean what is friendship for, man?)

OF COURSE, IN modern life, decoys no longer *mean* to draw southbound fowl down toward your waiting gun. I know that. But, robbed of that cocky junior wood duck meant as mine, I got grouchy about folk art generally. Started wondering:

When does "Americana" become that?

Carved ducks, once meant to help you feed your family, aren't they now just national good-luck charms? Find them on U.S. stamps or speckling wallpaper at inns. Only when decoys were outlawed after tricking too many birds to death did we find them fully "lovable" at last. (Regarding our handsome nation's future in the hungry world, is there not a *hint* here?)

Yes, I was pissed at losing my drake. Loyalty goes unrewarded when you're seen as one who'll stay no matter what. My leverage, if any? Canceling the Ropers' home owners' policy?

Miffed, silent, I decided it was really kind of odd anyway, trying to exactly imitate another living thing. Who'd *do* that? I mean, imagine if, say, all life-sized bronze figure sculpture got painted to look exactly like human beings. What if art museums left out beautiful half-naked lady-statues to try and lure living breathing young men indoors? And why? to trick, trap, kill and eat them? See my point?

I hurried home from the show, champagne-high in a way that made me feel, even walking, not quite balanced. Jan was kind enough not to ask if I'd got the one I'd set my heart on. As she settled before our usual nightly news, I told her I sensed one of my sinking spells coming, just needed a quick nap. Twenty minutes, tops. I went right down into a kind of suicidal sleep. Had this windy, saturated dream in color:

Imagine you are flying south, migrating, actually. You lead your airgroup and—with raw sun sinking quick—you keep scouting, seeking any inlet where your kind might settle, feed, rest.

Some memory of gunfire elsewhere keeps you circling the blue cove below. Others—behind and beside you—await your signal-dive. Only that will prove how all this under you is safe. You're tired and so are other flyers. But the inlet down there looks too ideal. True, some of your own sort already float there. Still, this might be a trick. But then you notice another one such as you. A more splendid example of your species, your sex. This male's already bobbing at his ease to one side, guarding his own thirty. Even from on high you note the drake's bold coloring, his bearing unflappable. And so, descending, bringing in your group to aim for water's surface nearest him,

you imagine greeting such a one. A fellow leader, his size notable, his mark-
ings almost . . . gunshots. Sharp pops, feathery explosions left and right.
Three fall, now four, as you ascend.

Beating upward, panicked, you sense at once: your group's undoing is
your own too-trusting need for another worthy's company. That's what got
four good ones killed back there. Your visible authority is really just your
own male loneliness kept perfectly hidden. That other leader? likely wood.
Unflappable, all right.

You, shaken, betrayed by your own kind, wing on. No loyalty. Not like
you, he cannot have been quite real. Resemblance itself can be stolen. Attrac-
tion? Lethal. Turns so quick against you. Can kill you and all of yours.

19

THE BIXBY TWINS, barely teenaged, had grown amazing-looking,
already built like anything. Their child faces were now carried around
atop these panther limbs. Boys knocked at our door, announcing
they'd be showing off their matched diving at the club, July Fourth.
Could we come? They were walking all over Riverside inviting old
friends. Sweet when kids that young still want to sit and talk to silver
oldsters like Jan and me. They asked by name about Jill and Billy,
though our kids had been years ahead of them in school.

Of course, we felt closer to the twins for having seen them go
underwater and drown powder-blue. I'd not forget pulling these
newts from our Lithium so someone else could fill them with his air.
You'd think the boys might ever-after find our river terrifying; but
no—absolute water babies.

At the club, twins greeted everyone. Barely fifteen, tanned completely dark, each wore a Band-Aid-sized black Speedo, a short hair-
cut exactly matching his brother's. Rumor had it they'd just "been
with" a handsome married lady of forty. Both with her at once, fore
and aft, it was said then immediately believed. Her husband spent
months away at tobacco market in Georgia. Turns out, most mar-

ried ladies her age can keep secrets far better than identical new-
bies, fifteen.

Riversiders' disapproval was offset by some awe at imagining the
sight. The Fallen imagined this woman corrupting our Tomothy-
Timothy concurrently; folks felt a hushed respect for her gall, her
sheer twofer enterprise. She had hired the boys for a fix-it job, "Come
help me clean my gutters?" Afterward, passing this put-together
lady at the mall, nobody quite issued her the "cut-direct." Instead,
freighted humid looks got offered. Especially by other women of a
certain age. Looks said, *How?* The *why* was understood. People all do
crazy things when it's their last-chance-ever. I told you, Riverside is
rarely unintentionally rude.

Presiding at Broken Heart's pool, Kate Bixby, the twins' glad
mother, played hostess and was gracious and dear despite all that
weight she's put on. (Why so unhappy, you think?) Luckily, the
forty-year-old seductress in question had the Protestant good sense
to stay away.

Tomothy and Timothy's mirror-image dives made us all feel
proud then stronger. People said they had a clear shot at the upcoming Atlanta Olympic trials. You could tell already: fond as we were
of them, Bixbys seemed destined to be among the Fallen who did
not stay.

Greetings at their diving demonstration made me feel a solid
part of Riverside. It was in the clubhouse bathroom afterward I got
another bulletin concerning me. It arrived in the usual way I seem to
learn: myself viewed via outside diagnosis, more than any deep personal reflection, hard as I try.

Shy, I'd chosen the farthest row of urinals. From there I overheard one of my favorite tennis partners at the sinks telling his chum,
"Yeah, we caught Bill Mabry with Mom, at home. Having tea. And
trying to sell her *flood* insurance! A hundred and fifty miles from the
ocean. And her always claiming she can't even afford new dentures.
Hers do whistle. And here he is sitting looking out at the ducks with
her, and pushing that. Brochures out, the works. Given Bill's history,

people feel for him. Don't think he doesn't use that pity in his business, too. But, trying and pile coverage onto someone Mother's age?
My sisters and I think he's overstepping."

NOW I HAD been shunned as a Marion collector eager to pay retail,
I can hardly overstate how shamed I felt. He had no idea what-all he
meant to me, but then did *I*? Losing that mere object, it left me truly
shaken, silently enraged, convinced I should possibly go rogue. Bill,
the Indie! I mean, how hard could it be? To take a hunk of wood and
make it be or go . . . duck-shaped? Just out of spite, I'd maybe start
with a wood duck. Where is it written that an able man retires to no
lifeline stronger than his cable news?

I avoided Bobbitt's Hobby Shop where the Roper fan club gathered. I made a trip to Raleigh I sort of hid even from Jan. There I
bought superlative German gear. "State-of-the-art everything," the
guy promised. Tomorrow I'd try my first one as an experiment. I'd
do it all in my tool shop where we keep grandkids' life jackets and
temperamental weed-eaters. Safe back there, even if I found myself a
slow starter, all thumbs, not even the wife need know.

As I might have said, the week our boy finished Haverford (with
high honors), Janet went out and bought herself a pair of cockatiels,
noisy seed-scatterers. She embarrassed me even more by naming
them for our now-absent son and daughter. But, today, for raw inspi-
ration, I did step into our kitchen, did stare into their cage. "Hi, Jill.
Hi, Billy." Real birds, after all, if unfit to ever model as matching
American wood ducks.

I retired to my shop-studio feeling pumped up, almost wicked,
granted a second and more sexual life. I'd once overheard my son tell
a pal how some choir girl lighting candles at All Saints made him
"get wood during service." That term, new to me, I found funny.

But now to business. Using my twelve hundred dollars of Kraut
engineering and tempered Sheffield steel, I would mold and make
it, major wood. I set the virgin cedar block into my bench vise,
secured it. *That's* not going anywhere. "Step One, Phase II. Completed, Houston."

TURNS OUT EVERYTHING my father possessed in anti-golfing talent, I'd inherited at anything artistic. It's not just about intelligence, is it? Within ten minutes I discovered an even deeper secret—lack of even any actual motor skill. (In your head, you can see a thing so clearly . . .) It remained my news alone; right till Jan had to drive me to the ER. Just eighteen stitches, really. Told Janet I'd been fixing the lawn mower. She grunted, *"That'd* be a first."

Next day, one hand mittened in gauze, I sneaked down to our river. I took that red-stained block and chucked it. Tossed my wood-handled Sheffield blades into our crooked little river. I recalled down-loading Red's handmade if subcontracted SHADOWLAWN sign. I enjoyed watching every darned item bobble off toward the Atlantic far far away.

We all have our gifts. —Don't we?

At Doc's exhibit I'd bent at the knees, I'd stared so hard into his glass case. I had felt pride that slid at once into longing. Shelves had mirrors behind them; cruel, that. You saw your own blocky stubbled face edging streamlined wildlife. "Sad" can sometime seem a default setting for our whole flock of the Fallen over sixty.

I kept replaying how he'd turned down my blank-check. My good-faith-offer for that little "me" bird, half-angel, half-juvenile delinquent. Grabbed by some poacher, it'd likely been shipped off to the City. Ransomed north, needing only my wad of cash to keep it here in Falls, a fellow stay-at-home. Doc's pip of a masterpiece, exiled to New York's East Side, institutionalized far from here and me. Atop some white Formica pedestal.

—Hoping for what? a museum or open water.

20

I'D FELT SO healthy being twenty-two, home with the framed Chapel Hill "bachelor of science." Beside it, in my insurance office, I hung the laminated "antiqued" certificate proving me also a licensed CPA.

Jan and I were just back from our honeymoon (Washington, D.C., for some reason). Partly educated, fully married and employed, I first claimed, then fought to hold, Doc's first Monday slot. If some hospital emergency took him elsewhere, I'd sometimes bob in anyway, joke around with his nurses. Hefty efficient Blanche and both funny Sandys. Same names, unrelated, they'd started saying they were sisters as a joke. Now they admitted sharing the same Clairol "Ash Blond" and it made them, in crisp white with folded caps, seem even cuter, almost-twins. I felt they counted on my turning up to get their week launched with a joke, good one, an old favorite.

Everyday sameness? At least it made life feel potentially longer. Right hand on the steering wheel, left on your emergency brake. By the standards of Eden, Falls' routes and habits might've seemed poky. But things flowed along as shallow yet easeful as our busywork Lithium itself. Insurance soon became clockwork, regularized and well-paying if in steady dribs and drabs. (I've always been a faster study than anybody else around here mostly cared to know.) By trade I was a cheerful seller of insurance. And I ensured I'd daily sell myself as a cheerful version of that. Call me a decoy 9–5. From my Fidelity notepad I summoned our national adjusters to sites of grease fires, fender benders. But Riverside somehow seemed exempt from maiming tractor-accidents, barn burnings, country gore.

EARLY SEPTEMBER IS my favorite time for outdoor exercise. Maples have started rusting that first mellow tint. Air along our river holds a crisp sort of start-of-school Granny Smith promise. So find me pounding away at the backboard of the Broken Heart tennis courts.

Even as a country boy of eight I preferred tennis to golf. The sight of my first court seemed like a perfect memory of order. Like those faint blue lines on school paper. Given my cardiac picture, I'd never be Wimbledon material. On my doctor's advice I tend to favor doubles but still love the game. Odd, I associate its pleasures with enjoying flossing my teeth. Nets? Strings? Always the constant cleanly sounds of tennis leave me feeling purified. Bit clearer in the head.

Dad admitted disappointment. My failing to take up golf hurt him, he admitted. Tennis seemed a gelded game to this ex-farmer, "You're practically indoors. Might as well play bridge." But, belief in Golf? it's like God—either you've always accepted it or, on sight, you find the very idea ridiculous. Those pompomed caps? men's pastel pants and shiny white shoes, the rickety length of the clubs and the sneaky size of that ball! From the start, all of it struck me as some visual joke designed by a real mean gay *New Yorker* cartoonist.

Red begged me to at least caddy for him. "I mean, we're lifetime legacy members and you are m' only begotten son, son." But Roper, noting our recent shortness of breath, had politicked us toward half-rounds. Doc knew how long it took poor Dad to chop across the course.

Red was running out of even unpopular partners. The oldest had found his game too slow, ragged, yet peppery. City veneer fell away as he cursed the pro's poor preparation of Red himself. By now Dad played through mostly alone. At golf, Red's usual workmanlike focus got outfoxed only by his comic lack of talent. "Address the ball," he'd say aloud, stepping toward it, as if trying to make a small if obstinate new friend.

This was a few years before our club required carts. They meant to keep foursomes moving at a new industrial pace. (Here lately, the Broken Heart Admissions Committee's been throwing open the gates to more and more retired New Jerseyites. Remaining dot-com money, certain loudish Johnny-come-latelies. A shame, really.)

Red had taken our doctor's advice years back. He now worked around the schedule of that revered senior caddy, Maitland "Mait" Miller. A skinny handsome blue-black man, Mait had very white hair. It grew in pleasing mossy coins set around his skull like some type of crown or cap. Red once joked: Mait had been "thinking the game" so long his hair had become all cotton golf balls.

As Doc promised, Mait's caddying gave the suave impression of someone never hurried. "Ball went in the drink? That do happen. Nothing worry 'bout. I got us another two dozen, dry, right here. Which one these looks luckiest?"

Maitland Miller served as deacon in his church, had a daughter at Reed. As old as he was, lank and nonchalant, he might've caddied for each justice who'd sat on the Supreme Court since William Howard Taft. Nowadays he might be a college president. Back then he helped white fellows whittle points off their "mental game" for life. Though they'd never seen him play, never once invited that, they trusted his every grunted hint and nod.

Doc Roper turned up at Broken Heart this same sunny day mid-week. From my backboard, I could see him yonder on our putting green, perfecting shot after shot with his usual directed patience. Roper's hair stood out up spiky white against clubhouse bricks. Like me and many players here today, Doc seemed constantly scolding himself with how-to's. "There you go at the elbow again, you." Had to laugh, imagining Doc making any public goof-up he couldn't at once correct.

I wondered if he'd glimpsed me over here punishing the back-board. (I always seemed more aware of where he stood than he of me.) Hoped Roper'd spy me exercising; that way I'd get points in his office early Monday. Always did try preparing some starter topic as I am told folks do for their weekly head-shrinkers.

It being a Wednesday noon, few other members were around; mainly waitresses in white watering petunias on our terrace, gossiping about some big upcoming Moose Lodge dance. You had a sort of peaceful backstage feeling. Nothing counted today. No one was looking. My vital signs felt vital and I was just twenty-two. How glad I was for my skinny candid Janet and our beautiful house full of her family antiques.

My essential players were all nearby: Doc, alone with his putting, giving at the knees as charts all show. Pop out somewhere, getting shaken-head sympathy from Mait at each bad shot. And here I was, pounding lethal serves against defenseless green plywood. I pictured Red chopping away but due back at one for our lunch buffet. He still swore by Broken Heart's oily fried chicken but seemed proud he'd cut down thanks to medical advice: just two drumsticks, one breast.

"That's *it*," a Christian martyr, Red would shove back from the table. I stood wondering if I might ask Doc to join us (hating to impose). I had turned his way when seeing something living rush across the greens.

What I first took for a deer turned into a man, a black man, then someone familiar. Mait Miller, minus any golf bag, advanced at whatever speed you could make in such long limps. He held something up above his head. A red bandanna. Spying him from this distance, knowing him to be over seventy-five, I wondered at his hurry, worried for his heart. Then I noticed he kept waving his hankie as some signal, running, stopping, waving, running, bending, winded. I noted Mait aim his flag always at Doc.

I screamed Roper's name while pointing. He scanned, saw, dropped his putter, took a running leap onto the club manager's cart, key in its ignition. I piled on behind. We were soon to Maitland at a sand trap's edge. He'd bent, hands to knees. The old guy stood huffing toward the grass.

"Is Mr. Red. He down on sixteen. He out. Made him one giant swing. I heard something turn. Break aloose. Not soft, wet. More like the handle popping off a china cup. Swear I heard something inside he chest just *go*."

We were there in two minutes. Red lay on his back staring up into a yellowed maple. He still clutched the aluminum club. His fists stayed fused around his iron's leather grip, pinkies linked as friends'd all tried teaching him.

Dirt on his forehead showed he'd first pitched facedown; Maitland had likely rolled him into a more restful position half against some maple roots. I squatted and touched Red's cheek. The day's temperature was right at fifty-five, and so was his. Eyes open wide, such a look lay starched across my father's face. Determination mixed with some incoming glory expected any minute. ("How was *that*?") I tried pressing shut his eyes but lids stayed fixed, amazed—from the inside out.

Doc, unceremonious, shoved me aside, checked Dad's airways,

tore open his shirt. The butt of Roper's right hand went slamming to work on him. Blows sounded harder than I liked but Doc knew best. I remembered Red's saying that here, in town, he did not always know how to behave, to "do." Me too, me now. Something would soon be called for, some emotion or efficiency. I studied how Doc pounded a human torso, punishing one organ to recall its duty and main habit. I, Bill, watched as if I were some camp kid in first-aid class, doubting I could ever do all that. (What real *use* was I to others?)

Maitland Miller wandered off, he acted the most upset. Kept mumbling, not quite to me, "Didn't mean nothing by it. Hates this part the job. Lost Mr. Alston, Judge Draper, then Mr. Blanchard Sharp went. They quit they jobs. Got plenty money left. But be out here every morning, still hurrying. I told Mr. Red, say, 'Go easy.' Then I run. But Mait ain't fast as Mait been being."

I broke the spell. Dared touch his arm. Promised Maitland he was the hero of the hour. Told him Dad had already outlived his own pop's span by twenty-odd years. I said that Mom and I would want Mait at Dad's funeral, please. I would talk to the manager. Maitland Miller had caddied for Red all these good last years. Dad gave famous tips because he finally could. That at least seemed fair.

Mait, shaking his head, walked off mumbling, red hankie to mop his brow. He settled on the far side of that maple, one live man and one dead. I saw cars start slowing out at the corner of Club and River. Given Red's hair color and bantam size, from there they'd know the fallen.

Somebody had phoned the rescue squad but our groundskeeper wouldn't let their ambulance ruin his greens. So here medics came, running their gurney around a sand trap, guys all in white showed up stark against this bright green world. I must've been stunned. Everything looked painted. Everything visible played a part in making this be one huge September show-day. No hiding place in it. Straight sunlight came at you, yellow as yolk, and warmed you; but blue shade on the back of your head pulled you off toward coolness. Left split, I turned around.

Our afternoon had just enough wind in it to make these old trees sound huge. Overhead sweeps and creakings of high limbs left me feeling boy-sized stuck down here among adults' odd chest-pounding ritual. Everything grand and serious. Me, extra, misplaced, in town.

I squatted nearer Doc still pumping. Beside my father's head I noted what first appeared a single mushroom growing in the grass. Bright and red and white, it rested amid fresh-chopped divots. Thing proved to be Pop's wooden tee and, atop it, the new white ball right where it'd started.

Doc Roper kept hunched over Red, delivering well-paced blows to a chest narrow and yielding. Dad's face, neck, hands had been forever sun-baked. Brown-red, they seemed carved from a mineral different than his body's. This chest looked decades younger, flour-white as any child's. Face-up he appeared trusting, awaiting some verdict, frail past even being dead. I noticed odd red patches crossing him—collarbones to ribs, a raw mass, overlapping starfished shapes. Some old scars? bad new tattooing? Slow, I understood these hundred savage tender marks were Roper's handprints.

Astride Red, Doc still slammed so. I can yet hear that sound, ribs' giving like nautical rope under stress. Bent now beside our doctor, I warned myself not to betray one childish emotion here, much less girlish ones. Hated disappointing Roper. We had dreaded this so long, and here, as he predicted, it was happening. Had happened.

I could see Doc's jaw set, profile neutral if distorted asymmetrical from his fighting back tears. The EMS boys had long ago strapped an oxygen mask onto Red. Now they stood back and aside. They'd recognized Roper at a hundred yards. Their waiting acknowledged he outranked them. But, twenty minutes in, they started giving each other looks, phoning bulletins to one irked supervisor. Someone else, alive, needed help now. It was clear my dad was dead. Seeing Doc's pace slow some, one young medic finally helped Roper rise. He'd worked with such force he appeared briefly weak, even tipsy, arms flung out for balance. Doc lurched off to one side, his back turned, avoiding a short form being lifted to its stretcher.

Doc leaned against one tree as I moved to comfort or thank him or maybe report how this shock was registering with *my* ticker! But Roper turned on me as if outraged. Under damp white hair I saw those strange blue eyes fried open.

"Nothing. Could do nothing. And Red, he'd just asked me to play-through with him. Maybe I could've slowed him some, Bill? But, no, I had to be working on my stupid putting which will never be worth shit anyway. Bill? how hard would it've been? My tagging along no matter how much *time* it took? —Well, we're not going to let this happen to *you*. Advances made every day. You're twenty-two. I swear I'll keep right up. And you there with me, son. I hate this for you. Everybody despised Paxton. He snitched on every woman he ever had. Man robbed anybody ever tried fixing up that barn of his. But, you know? his choosing Red to make an heir? that was the coolest thing he ever did. Red! Pleasure just being around somebody finally wringing the real *fun* out of stuff, you know? Sure you do. But, know this, you're *my* guy now. Umkay? I hate his going. But, swear to God, I've *got* you now."

Doc gripped my right hand; I returned his exact caliber of male force till we sort of stood here Indian-wrestling. Soon we actually on-purpose hurt each other, part of our pact to make this stick. Being Red's two all-time favorite young men, being out here under the maples on sixteen, we finally seemed more than brothers. The man swore he'd keep me going years longer than he'd managed with our Red. And, till today at least, my partner Roper, he's honored his promise, hasn't he?

BEFORE I EVEN phoned my bride at our new home, I drove straight to Mom's. I later realized, by the time she heard my car out front, not his, she knew. No, earlier. See, somehow she'd already changed into her best black Sunday dress. Matching black shoes. Hair pulled back then pinned. No brooch. Nothing but a wedding ring. In town, she knew to keep it simple, solid colors. Otherwise they might know. So, always understate. Today especially.

As I lunged in, she rose. Just the sight of me still in sweaty tennis whites made her lean against the doorjamb and ask it: "Where?"

"On sixteen."

"Ooh and after he promised me he'd quit at nine. But you're not *with* him. You let him go. Son, where have they *got* Red?"

"Downtown, wherever ambulances wind up. We'll find him, I'll take you there. But, look, sweetheart, Doc was right with him. Tried heart-massage, just tried and tried. So Dad had the best last chance."

"Well, there it is." She sat again then turned away from me. I felt she was cross that he had died with me, not her.

"First, Bill, you'll run home. Change out of those shorts. Tell Janet and don't even say you came told me first. She's your wife now. Go to her. And, son, I reckon we'd best start. Been so long coming, hasn't it? There's certain things'll now need doing."

I stepped closer to stop her, to explain how all this other could wait. But she held up one palm. I saw she needed to say out her little speech. *Let her*, I told myself but the sound of the voice in me saying that seemed exactly Red's.

Her fine white skin showed against everything black. Right then she was such a beautiful woman, my mother. I stood here appreciating her with a licensed force that shocked me. I felt my strength had somehow doubled. Inheritance. With Red and his dear noise stopped, she came across as someone so poised and clear, kind. At seventeen, she'd married him knowing exactly what waited. Today I finally saw her just as he did and it offered such a wild pure charge.

"I'll want this place sold, Bill. My sister she's been after me to move back out to her farm in and with her, time comes. Time's here, I reckon. Yeah, be moving in with Ida. She's always had that spare room, ground floor, two nice windows. So I'll be there mainly. Look, from here on out, son, you might find me less in a town mood. Never really took to Falls. Except for Third Baptist, can't seem to feel relaxed here. It was Red's little side-trip, with us all trying and fit in and act like the Fallen. But it sure did suit my men. With me? Didn't like to say a word again' it, not back then. Not after he kind of *won* Falls like a prize. But I never left off being 'country.' And it's not one thing wrong with that. Look what I've got myself wearing here! They choose clothes like they upholster their couches. Black. Got me where I'm looking like a nun. But once I'm out with Ida, hiding with just us, why, I'll want to wear any ole floral-print housedress. Bagged-out, missing buttons? Should I care? Shoes run-down in back. That used to be luxury for me and m' folks. So, you go get your wife and carry her back over here once you've changed. White shirt'd be nice, jacket, no tie. See? here I am . . . him dead, worried how we'll look downtown at their offices."

She rose again and called me over, nearer her face, as if to whisper some new secret. I leaned in, finally put one arm around her. Against my cheek she whispered, "Oh, Bill, what are we going to do without our wonderful friend?!"

I shook my head. No answer.

But a new thought of hers now seemed to cheer Mom. "Well, there's one thing's sure. You and me we'll go right-today, we'll find him a mighty nice plot. —A *'town'* grave. Right, son?"

I HOPED TO wangle for Red a spot in All Saints Episcopal's moss-green churchyard. One ancient magnolia canopies its marbled lambs and man-sized angels. Buried there are presidential candidates and Secretaries of the Navy. Of course, this being Falls, oldest families monopolize its real estate, too.

Red, he'd never dared set foot into this famous church itself; it meant too much to him. I knew as how graveyard slots here ran real scarce and pricey. You could not just be One Who Stayed, however noble your local existence. But, since Janet's family had belonged to All Saints since Millard Fillmore's day, I thought Red might get grandfathered in yet again. I hated the beggar's role but sat down, took deep breaths, forced myself to phone.

Rector Tim's secretary was an English war bride with one posh and pearly accent. "Yes, All Saints. How might I help you?" Her formal voice slowed me some. The words "All Saints" seemed kind of exclusive, in fact, pure dare. I hate name-droppers. And here I was about to beg for something impossible, just to say I'd tried. "No, you can't," I answered, hanging up.

I'd lacked the brass to become a diplomatic climber even in my grief. Still too pending a person, I couldn't even *fake* Dad's natural push. Even to get him safely under hallowed ground.

So Mom and I, grave-wise, we just went with First Presbyterian. True, their flat memorial park allows "no aboveground flowers." Yeah, it's located more out toward the Dairy Queen. It lacks antique magnolia cover and is too new but still, pretty enough, maintained. Besides, Red had tithed Presbyterian, so they were fine having us.

I SAT UP that night of the day he died. Sat trying to write a gravestone-text sufficiently poetic. Funny, Jan had wanted to stay up with me and I appreciated that, her level head for confronting trouble straight-on. But I told my wife I had to do this part alone.

A beautiful antique writing desk overlooks the river in our great room, a bird's-eye maple thing with carved feet and from Jan's family plantation. But it seemed too fancy for my chore. Describing other people is a big responsibility, especially at the end. I moved around our place, holding open the blank back pages of my insurance premium book. The pad that usually only notes others' car wrecks, trees fallen into friends' homes. I wandered my own house, some overawed visitor among my wife's grand things. And the one workspace that felt easiest proved Lottie Clemens's cubbyhole off our utility room.

My task needed a place carved out for taking work-hour breaks. When Lottie Clemens cleaned for us and looked after things, she had her own backstage changing room between the washer-dryer and the pantry. Lottie daily arrived in civvies and shifted in and out of her uniform here before we drove her home. I noted her headquarters had a narrow daybed, an armoire, one massive iron hat rack that she'd hung with folding umbrellas and clear rain bonnets to protect her expensive braided hairdos. Thumbtacked before the card table, school photos of her four sons, the eldest grinning under high-school mortarboards. Lottie called it her office and it was a simple functional room and the only place in our fine split-level river-view house I felt somehow close to Red. Tonight it looked like a room at a farm.

Here I'd face the simplifying work of trying to see him whole. Here, for the first time, I felt like an only child. He had always seemed, in his forward-leaning belief, someone roughly my age. First I made a sort of poem filling two pages of insurance premium ledger; it went long and stayed bad. Bad country Baptist sentiment. I knew that, but still settled right into it, rolled around there, like a dog in the carcass of dead wildlife. Then I tore all that up and hid it in one sweater pocket.

Finally, feeling plainer in this staging area where our good help weekly prepared herself to help us, I went more country-sensible. I grew more manly, recalling the sheer city-expense of carving too many letters into marble. Finally I got it somewhat shortened. By dawn, in Lottie's office, I sensed I had it.

William Rooney Mabry II
1924–1975
Citizen

21

DAD'S FUNERAL WAS right well-attended. Leading families who couldn't come sent idled older cousins or those servant-helpers who'd dealt with Red most directly. Marge and Doc rode with us. Ten dark cars arrived in a divided convoy, his redheaded relations quick to stand far far apart. Separate glaring groups, Hatfields and McCoys. Had to be the "Peanut" Mabrys vs. the "Sweet Potato" ones. They looked cousinly as Israelis and Palestinians, that likely being half the trouble.

Red, alone among Mabrys, failed to be counted among those that stayed. Somehow he'd found the nerve to light out for town. And by gosh, Red had plowed out a place for himself and his blood, right here among the mightiest Fallen, verily even along The River Road. So, two clans' arriving "en masse" while still warring, gave best proof of this burial's being (strictly locally, of course) a state occasion.

Maitland Miller and his heavyset wife turned up by cab. They kindly refused to sit with Mom and Jan and Doc and Marge and me but seemed to appreciate the thought. Along with Mait and his Mrs., four of our younger caddies appeared up, edgy, scanning with stage fright this big a white church. They were quick to find me and Doc, to shake our hands, praising Red. "He been one the only *real* ones out there."

All dressed today in black suits and white shirts, their rich skin sleek as if oiled, they didn't seem the nicknamed youngsters from our clubhouse. Not in their flashy shirts, freed from lugging old white men's bags, today, on a rear pew picked by them, lined up to honor Red, their wariness gave them a strictness and reserve. They could've been the young Oxford-educated presidents of emerging African nations.

I'D PHONED RIVERSIDE'S best lady-realtor about selling Mother's Cape Cod. Mom stood listening in. The agent, as if expecting me, snapped, "Fine, but I could not even think of showing you-all's little place with its existing-colored doors and shutters."

So, one week after the funeral, I gave myself the chore. Knowing it would prove winding, I'd have to pace myself. Couldn't bear to hire another man for such a private duty.

Mom, already become the total hider, knew my chore. She dodged both that and daylight, deep indoors.

I took thick, plain enamel to his brighter choice.

"Red," I said as I drowned it all in white.

THE MONDAY AFTER Friday's burial my usual checkup was slated and I kept it and Roper breathed as usual to warm his stethoscope's steel and listened to me dutiful front-and-back and finally patted my shoulder but neither of us said one word the whole time, not daring to. It would be very hard if any or all of the emotion got out. I didn't trust myself. As usual, I chose to wait. *When till, Bill? Wait for what? Dignity, Revelation, Legacy? Love? To wait for Later: that seemed my major inborn task.*

I simply sat there on an exam table that had seemed both Dad's and mine, sat here singly.

I knew that the twenty-seven thousand dollars' profit we'd made selling his house would please Red very much. Three days after the funeral Mom already lived out in the country with her widowed sister. They themselves had wallpapered "her" room, giggling at every difficulty of gooped paste and paper's rolling corners. Its pattern proved both sprigged and striped, featuring giant purple lilac blooms. It was certainly a print no Riversider would ever have used, even in some "for the fun of it" chauffeur's garage-apartment's half-bath. I knew that Mom was in on this joke, to some extent. Of course I didn't press it. Clear, she'd never again live in any room painted just one tasteful color.

I stayed on in Falls, of course. But as a former farm kid, I never could feel town-born. I was never a soul fully local anywhere but halfway, about where the tobacco field around our Dairy Queen stands. Brilliant? No. And not gifted with any one particular skill past trying out a million silent decencies. I found most of those had gone sort of unnoted. That left me what? Whom? Where? Left me here.

"Having stayed" became a Purple Heart, for meritorious immobility. And likely I would stay on here where too little happened but the usual subtraction. Now "stay" meant being grounded by my father's grave. The Presbyterians kept it trimmed with Presbyterian efficiency, leaving me little to do but stand there and look down at it.

But, however uneasy I am about my achievements in life, if only in secret, I do give myself this: In the privacy of my heart, telling no one ever, some evenings looking back on my own better sort of days, I'll tell myself, fully meaning it: I admit that my father found me noble, gifted, a naturalized Riversider almost royal. And so, if only in his eyes, I do stay that: the sole surviving son and heir to the happy Earl of Shadowlawn.

2 2

BY NOW, IF, vacationing, you mentioned your hometown, the name of a certain craftsman might buoy up. His hand-hewn second-career had got so much press, even strangers asked if you'd seen, possibly even *met*, him? The retired doctor was now richly established as "Marion, carved by his hand ©."

Though also getting along in years, Doc looked little different from when he retired. He changed so slowly and that made him freakish, if also more a sort of good-luck tribal totem-pole. Only Marge had aged, maybe lacking a passion on the order of Roper's. You cannot get that by decoy-proxy.

I should know.

You can tell I'm heading toward the trouble. Not that we have not had bumps already. But no good story is a story only everyday. All of us only get away with just so much and then only for so long. Even in a moneyed river town, even someplace whose water is part amber lithium, part clear nicotine, life can retract its promise overnight. Can become a vale of tears breaking over you its sudden lashing. We had named ourselves "Falls," copying Niagara (no truth in advertising there!). Maybe we were about to pay for stealing the Big-Time's thunder?

These were our end-days, looking back. The time Before. And Roper might or might not turn up at others' cocktail parties. That depended on how "tacky" the paint felt on his "maybe all-time breakthrough coot." Doc overexplained the merits of everybody's Internet. You'd think he had invented it, boasting he could blow up any colored bird-image, could magnify then graph it to many times actual size. Did we actually *care*?

Sometimes at the club or downtown, you still caught sight of him. The guy no longer wore his reassuring after-hours witch-doctor's pendant, the stethoscope. Lately a jewelers' loupe shone, clipped to his tortoiseshell reading specs. He did pretty detailed work and, after all, the guy was now up over eighty.

Times, I longed to take him aside and sit and reminisce about our Red. As you'd get to swap tales only with a favorite sibling. To do that while on a camping trip, off canoeing up the Lithium, would be great. Just starting every sentence, "Remember that time Red . . . ? and that crazy time our dad, he . . . ?"

IT WAS IMPOSSIBLE not to respect Doc, so long-established here; but then, our witch-doctor, he held out—silent—for even more. Didn't withhold anything, exactly. But you feared he might. So you yourself made up the difference. For him, you produced a certain unreciprocated low-grade feeling; you forced it into something stronger, more bulked-up, yet your effort was still unimpressive. It finally felt humiliating, the strange suspense he exacted from the likes of ordinary me. Did he flirt with anyone? And, if not, why did everyone believe themselves the first?

How many women in his office had—like Kate Bixby that day her boys drowned then lived—offered more, all? But Doc never seemed to take free samples. And this just drew more offers. Roper seemed to barely notice us while off-duty; and yet, he always assumed our full infirm attention anywhere he went. Still, something kept a person coming back.

ESPECIALLY AFTER RED died in our company, it seemed Doc's company alone met some basic medical need of mine. "First, do no harm." That in itself is a mouthful. Roper's river-swim each dawn across from my place had simply seemed what any good doctor would do for his nearest patient. That Australian crawl left me still sitting nice and dry on my deck and yet feeling half-flooded with borrowed pheromones. I cannot explain it. Nobody was alone in feeling this, I swear. The list of locals that Doc had saved soon seemed the roster of home owners under eighty-five. We all still had these immense riverside houses, echoing louder since our kids had somehow grown and gladly moved; but the houses, for all their costs and repairs, still looked beautiful to us. Monuments, but honoring what? Still, as much else failed, ownership gave us its own time-release back-channel consolation.

Doc had forever known that facts about his other patients would fascinate us. Doc stayed rightly stingy with those. But a hunk of log carved so its "head" tucks under its "wing"? Could that ever rival news of whether polio would let the Collier girl ever walk again? Doc failed to note that life outranks art every time.

His poor Margie was left joking: "The man eats, sleeps, drinks ducks. I'm not a golf widow. I married a doctor, got a quack." *He'd* probably made that up, but she retailed it as her apology for him. People laughed at such a joke only because we'd always loved her. Good sport, Marge. Incredible rangy soccer player during her Randolph-Macon years. And once, when Doc was away at a Miami wood-tool convention, a Cambodian girl from the old mall's new nail place turned up at the Roper house seeking him, her waters just broken. Marge got the girl down in a porch lounge chair and delivered the baby herself. "All in a day's . . ." she said with that tough half-masculine tone of hers. Soccer captain, even at eighty. I'd noted that, as Roper and I got spindlier, somewhat artistic (spiritually in my case), our wives sort of toughened up, division of labor; Jan and Marge doubled down as stronger, more the bosses. To me they each looked a notch or two more bowlegged like poor Red. The pink razors along the bathtub's ledge? seemed there less for removing feminine leg stubble than possible new growth on their handsome chinny-chin-chins. But maybe this is sour grapes from a failing male whose actuarial life had never been long.

We sensed that, like us, Marge felt left a bit high and dry.

Roper'd never had an excess of the office-hour small talk we all craved like niacin, B-complex. Now? Any stray encounter in Sears' power-tool department started and quit with one of his mute nods. Retired, he seemed to have departed the office hours of language.

People had seen his canoe ashore and far upriver, his little brown tent pitched for some overnighter. Him alone, selfishly alone. Binoculars, a camou-parka and one fierce glance from Doc must mean: my trusty rusted Evinrude was disturbing some important-species-nesting-habitat he alone could guard.

Roper no longer seemed just absentminded. That'd been scariest when our village's weakening ventricles preoccupied the guy. Now he looked clear past your head, as if startled by your hair? no, he was squinting beyond, at what? oh, that red EXIT sign.

He would rather be sculpting. Even his rare jokes now seemed a pocketful of carving tools that might cut you mid-hug.

Was around this time that I, having washed out as a carver myself (healing nicely, if with certain scarring Doc would not have left), considered paying retail for a real Josiah Hemphill. The Christie's catalogue had one coming up. But I soon understood this was just my way to get Doc over to our place. A Hemphill, he'd come see. Pretty crude, I decided. One jerky decoy of a chess move. I was simply trying to pay for a last live visit from my real old friend, if he'd ever truly been one.

—How come I could send to a Manhattan gallery and acquire some Federal-period Hemphill but not get one brand-new across-the-road "Marion"? During my ever-shorter daily walks, I wondered this. (Sometimes to the point of muttering aloud.) The route of my daily constitutional? Past whatever home now lacked dogs that barked at me. Little slights, even from store clerks, preoccupied me. I kept casting back for reassurance. Found myself remembering, when I'd hitchhiked home from college, I once sat reading a translation of *The Odyssey* near our pool at Broken Heart. Doc, already 31, tanned dark as oiled teak, had gone off the high-dive, jackknifing midair. Amazing swimmer.

My own body gave signs it itself wanted to retire. From any strenuous further use. I could still drive a car anywhere. And I was a much safer driver than Jan liked to complain. Her jokes had always cast herself as Sensible and me as Her Dreamer. Like my true-believer dad, I guess. But artist at what? Which dreams exactly? Fame? Sex? Love? Elsewhere? After several enough drinks, Janet now did party-stand-up about my myopic U-turns and increasing inability to think in Reverse. But once I'd got us into the mall lot, once there, my even getting *out* of the car was something you might not want to watch too closely. I had seen my dad do this slow dance with himself at fifty-one. Made me think of a bug on its back, six legs scrambling, grabbing for doorframe, anything to gain the traction needed to get this creature pulled to the vertical. Then, having risen, for your trouble, another visa problem awaited, finding yourself at the next barricade, short of usable air. I sent my Janet on ahead, told her to go into Restoration Hardware and wait by their lamps. Jan was always drawn to their antique-y look but never bought one. She complained, "They *still* look too new." I told her, "Oh, I can do that. Can 'antique' it in my wood shop." "How, may I ask?" She sounded exhausted with knowledge of me.

"By *touching* it," I said. Which made her blanch then cackle. "I love you, you are so *sick*, Bill." By now, that had become her compliment! Let my Janet laugh.

I can handle anything but pity.

MY WIFE'S COLLEGE roommate came to visit every other year for "Kaye's beauty rest." She'd come fresh from divorce court again, her newest face-lift mended upward unevenly.

Kaye is smart in ways our little town cannot let itself be: she is witty and unforgiving *out loud*. Jan and I enjoy her company more than she knows, maybe more than she quite deserves. Kaye is old tobacco money and has what some people call style and others call edge. Kaye inherited enough, then married even more, three times running; so she always says exactly what she thinks in real-time. That, it seems, is no strict guarantor of happiness.

After weekend drinks enough, Kaye even gets *us* sounding like her. She would be leaving tomorrow for Barcelona because somebody she knew was free to have a luncheon there late Thursday. Jan and I marveled. But we, un-jet-lagged, felt blessed at this age to count ourselves among those that stayed aground. —No local guessed what-all terrible we'd just been confiding to Kaye. And God knows, that many gins in, *she* wouldn't remember.

I stood gladly preparing a second pitcher of dry dry Bombay Sapphire martinis. I'd swing these libations out onto the deck to heighten viewing tonight's already-terrific sunset.

Couldn't help overhearing our sophisticated guest quiz my wife, "Gosh, Jan? Who is that looking at a heron through binoculars and with no shirt? And here I thought Randolph Scott was extinct. Handsomest thing breathing. What is he, about fifty-eight? Looks to be on safari. Just my type and I never even knew that *was* a type. Seeing how I'm finally free of my fat dear oilman Roy, that'd be perfect for me. Who *is* the man?"

"That's not a man, dear, that's 'Doc.'" Janet coughed a laugh, one slightly bitterer than I ever liked others to hear. "And he'll turn eighty-two come June. There are parties already planned. Sad to say for you and others, there is a *Mrs.* Safari. The two're so happily married— they've upset many of us with daily comparisons. Doc there used to be our doctor, did wonders for Bill's heart. Miracles, in fact. But that eventually bored Doc. (Me, I think the ole alpha-bird lost his power when he lost his patients but he doesn't know that yet.) Now he's becoming a famous artist of sorts. Craftsman, anyway. So, you see, dear, he's not *just* a man. He sort of pokes up in the middle of us, kind of a weather vane. People tend to read the wind by *him*. I really think there's something wrong with him. Women want to save him so they can later be saved by him. And even men, otherwise intelligent men, they . . . well, I don't know *what* they want from him. But I've certainly shuddered picturing it. Roper over there makes everybody think things are better than they are. He promised Bill's sweet dad that he was tending the poor guy's subpar heart, no problem, good as new. But guess who dropped dead, practically in front of our medicine man? (*But where* is *my Bill with another several of these?*) In the end, Doc never seems to make any of it stick. Not exactly leading people on, more like writing prescription IOUs. But everything he promises is, it's . . . undeliverable. You know how they call certain guys confidence artists? Well, he does look good on paper, but . . . underneath there's something very puritan, starved-out. He's like a good copy of something that was, God knows, probably lots better coming out of the gate. —Meaning just the sort of guy all local women fall in love with . . . and I mean all! Plus about half our weaker men."

Amused, then surprised, I had started out, holding our best silver tray, its crystal pitcher full.

I saw we needed extra olives.

I turned back.

BOOK TWO

A.D.

APERSON'S PARENTS LABOR MIGHTILY TO PLACE THAT person on top-drawer waterfront land in the neighborhood where, if you cannot crawl home from tonight's cocktail party, you might just dog-paddle. What happens next will seem to surge from nowhere. That's just how it swept in on us house-to-house.

Person lives in a neighborhood called Riverside since age eight. Person assumes that the muddy inching little trickle rich with lithium will stay put like that store-bought background noise meant to help uneasy sleepers finally doze.

Yonder river should provide contrasting color for your Bermuda grass against its slow brown bend. It should not "say nothin' and just keep rollin' along." It is meant to offer a few annual edible grandkid-caught sunfish and shad. The shared neighborhood water feature seems dug to help you teach your kids sportsmanship in boating.

First came a hurricane named Gretel. Fierce winds had been predicted. Never gusted much past 50. It ain't even a hurricane if it drops to 74. Since *H* follows *G*, jokes ran we should fear brother *Hansel* next. As usual, we felt we'd got off pretty easy, at least in this more desirable part of town. All of Riverside went to bed after one more than our standard several drinks. We slept soundly, having ducked another biggie.

But, though we slept so well, we soon would wake to trouble, friend, right here in River City.

THE FIRST JAN and I recognized something was off we heard our birds Billy and Jill going berserk downstairs. That would have been about three a.m. The cockatiels Jan had foolishly bought then named for our absent kids to offset "empty nest" feelings? they squawked like the devil. Janet sits up saying, "What's got into them? Storm was a fizzle. I'll just go check, Billy. Remember how that one mouse spooked them so?"

Pitch-black-dark, and Jan climbs off the edge of our four-poster, opens the door into the hall. She wanders to our staircase and is half-way down before I hear her turning my way. Janet's usual calm governs every word. "Billy. Billy? There's . . . Our birds might just be *drown*ing."

Well, *that* got me up.

YOU ACCEPT AS how things will change but never overnight. You expect the mercy of a little slowness. I put on bedroom slippers and a silk robe as if it were Christmas morning and I'm just going down to photograph the kids opening their Santa loot. But tonight, to wander downstairs and to be suddenly wading. To slush, arms lifted, into your dark dining room. To "ford" your dining room. Then you hit something smelling like a badly-kept kennel and strangers' motor oil making one wrong mix. And all arrived here, silent, since you went to sleep among your fellow Fallen. That the water in your house feels river-cold seemed logical enough; far creepier, these stripes of warm. God knows what's fomenting in this chemical slop. It seems a Hell rehearsal, with water being fire. Its lithium does not cut our shock tonight. You descend into a house become aquarium. It offers further practice at your getting good at saying goodbye. Bye-bye to property, so long responsibility, and finally, maybe, solid earthen matter itself. "Dust to dust" is at least tidier than "Dust to mud."

Heroic, I waded into our kitchen and, idiotic, turned on each non-

working light-switch. Lucky for us there was most of a moon, and
it made everything go silver, mercury. Caged birds still kept going
crazy and then I saw it. Something swimming near them, circling
our marble-topped "island." I blindly found a broom and prodded
toward what seemed a black beaver-otter paddling hard. One hissing
yowl proved this must be the Blanchards' Siamese cat. How it had
washed into our home, I couldn't guess. I saw why Jan's birds were
freaking out. But, eating something feathered seemed the last thing
a cat this wet might crave.

"Jan, honey? We've got the Blanchards' *Tang* or *Chang* in here
swimming laps." "*Ming*," she corrected. Then we had the comedy of
my trying to save a drowning pet so irritated it would kill you for
getting it above the waterline. Finally I found Jan's thickest oven
mitts and, holding this thrashing oil-blackened creature far from me
head-outermost, I heaved it up on top of the fridge. It did not sound
real grateful there.

No, we counted ourselves among the lucky ones, really. Because
of a river hillside, our home stands three stories, not Riverside's usual
two. We soon sat on our roof beside caged cockatiels wet and noisy.
We sat between two dresser drawers stacked with family photos,
stock coupons; Janet's laptop (couldn't find its case). It contained the
all-important will. Brilliant, I was about to leave all my heart meds
lined neat along our bedside table. Quite a night then day ahead. Of
course, first thing, I checked across the street.

Doc and Marge's place showed no flashlight glare, no sign of life.
They'd likely already made a James Bond motorboat escape, somehow without asking us along. I had the bass boat but Janet worried that wrestling with that and even getting my reliable Evinrude
cranked would overtax me. At first I defied her. Got down into it
finally, worried if the short rope still securing it to our underwater
dock would hold. The Evinrude called "Old Reliable" for years would
not turn over. No way. It was dead and I had my omen. And Jan had
her first of several thousand *I told you so's.*

If our dear neighbor Mitch (my friendly insurance competitor) hadn't motored past right then in his aluminum outboard, I think we might still be perched up there at the roofline like birds ourselves. Our cockatiels, even on a good dry day, are ill-tempered, very irritating pets. They *do* nothing. Janet bought them without consulting me, right when our second kid went off to school. "They were on sale, two for the price of one. They're married, the clerk said." "Well, in that case." Next Jan made both of us seem even more conventional: by naming the male for Bill, Jr., and the girl for our brilliant linguist daughter, Jill. And I never once complained. Too much to even say.

When you lose everything overnight you gain at least surprising information. After that first gulping "Uh-oh," there can come a start-up giddiness. It registers almost as relief. Maybe only a man as old as I would think: *No more hiring teenagers to overpay for grass-mowing.* I'd come to hate our enslaving acre and a half! And to think how much my dad had valued a green yard of no farm-animal food value. If Red grew up fantasizing about town, my dreams had lately run toward a silent farmhouse, Presbyterian-plain, zero-maintenance—it would hold me, seated cross-legged alone on the plank porch, a Zen-monk hayseed whose only crops would be invisible hanging garden meditations.

Washed out, I imagined myself if Dad had not inherited. What if we'd been forced to apply for club membership using only my own looks and cash? If I lived in the country, would it be this wet? But I learned at once to try and hide any such idle speculation from my wife.

Most of our antiques downstairs had come from "Barton," Janet's mother's family's Edenton plantation. Me, being a tenant farmer's son, I'd inherited no object of importance. The Mabrys' everything had been provisional as next month's rent. The importance of Barton's 1799 sideboards and wing chairs to Jan would prove far greater than I'd ever even guessed.

Sounds absurd to say my wife mistook such farm furniture for the missing plantation itself. Might seem silly to admit how the loss of one slave-made cypress breakfront would give my unsentimental darling a nervous breakdown. But that is really sort of just what was about to happen.

2

WE (AND SIX hundred others) spent that first night in a National Guard armory. If its gym made for an unsightly B&B, at least the price was right. No friends could take us in, being flooded out as we. Many humans endure Some One Night When Everything Changes. Somehow, we, the Fallens' 6,803, all drew September 15th.

The richest people in Falls occupied Riverside's twelve square blocks surrounding us, ours. Falls' poorest folks live at sixes-and-sevens down near the closed cotton mill in B.A., Baby Africa. Its stretch of silt land has always been considered so worthless, freed slaves were given it for free. So, into this overlighted army multipurpose room, all us river rats crawled, finally together.

Whatever our class or race, we lugged the selfsame items: family Bibles, deeds, love letters, photos of dead parents, of living children and grandkids. We held our damp pets shivering inside bath mats, pillowcases. For once, we did not just nod howdy; we looked each other square in the eyes. Mait said, "Now, ain't this a bitch, Mr. Bill?" Here he stood, Dad's calming caddy. Miller's hair looked even whiter, with good reason. Almost before I knew quite who he was, Mait, greeted this evening, seemed a dear old friend. Think of all we'd been through together.

I asked, "You-all swamped, too?"

"Pretty much it got everything. And right when I had worked my yard up to where I could just about *look* at it." He studied the floor.

WE NONE OF us appeared our tip-top best, I promise you. In this gym crisscrossed by cots, echoing yapping dogs and crying kids, you heard a jumpy madcap energy short-circuited. You heard an intentional costume party's loudness. Everybody talked too loud and all our info came through eavesdropping, but at least we were alive. Half the children underfoot kept "acting out" unsupervised; the rest, in corners, stayed bent in thumb-sucking, fetal positions.

We bunched here imagining how it'd happened, to be attacked from the rear, our placeholder waterway gushing suddenly with Mississippi ambitions.

The "Why?" we'd leave to helpless half-drowned rectors to explain. The "How?"—our government should've known and warned us.

We sat on our provided cots, Vietnam surplus, stating common knowledge: the weather'd lately changed; hurricanes more frequent and far meaner. These days officials had to name so many storms a year they used up every English letter clear to X. Then they reverted to a second alphabet, the Greek one. (That in itself sounded a bit un-American.) Meanwhile the right-wingers in D.C. still ask each other, "Is there *really* global warming? Surely we need another blue-ribbon study." Republicans must not watch as much Weather Channel as Jan and I do in our rooted waning years.

The wife and I found, among other milling refugees, Lottie Clemens, our retired longtime child-care friend and cleaner. In her housecoat pocket, I saw a zip-lock bag full of costume jewelry. We seemed to be meeting on some train speeding toward the same internment camp. "The house! How the *house?*" She yelled for news of a place she'd weekly vacuumed forty years. Janet and I glanced at each other, then simplified our answer. We spared everyone's dignity by skipping details. We just shook our heads no.

"Don't be telling me that now. Unh-unh. Not the *house* . . ."

"But, Lottie, your boys?"

"Oh, they safe. Youngest two running round here somewhere. Both that age where they all-the-time playing they don't know me. Even while sitting there facing they own momma in the same *boat!*"

Then we kissed each other. I sort of cried all over Lottie—pillow breasts and wiry arms—she fell against and between us. With our last formality and feeble manners shot, we re-understood. Our lives, our childbearing years and these longer hot-flashing ones, our whole life spans had been spent together in one shuttling station-wagon and those same few rooms. Rooms now ruined. Including, I belatedly noted, Lottie's useful office.

—I vowed then, if we ever got through this I'd enlarge her pension. She is a decent funny woman with four sons, twelve grandkids, all somehow boys. (And I did live to boost her retirement. I'm not bragging. My truly stepping up to actually financing her old age, it was already overdue about four years.)

THE SMALLER THE town, the bigger the event looms. Or so I told myself. But the scale of both seemed huge tonight. The Department of Interior raffles off the wetlands meant to absorb our runoff rain. With Wal-Mart parking-lots paved hard, no sponginess is left. Water's got to go *some*where, so it came picking our locks. We all sat discussing this as someone said, "If I told you you were about to see Diana de Pres without makeup, would you believe me? Miracles and wonders." We turned, and the men, tired and old as we felt, somehow, helping each other, stood. If only saluting the memory of first seeing her enter a club dance eons back.

RIVERSIDE'S GREATEST CAUCASIAN beauty of our age, the witty bourbon-loving Diana de Pres, dragged our way, chuckling. "Well, this is what's left of the goods, boys," and she did a runway turn, witty in ruin. It still registered as sexy. Force of habit from all sides.

She stood blinking in not-good light wearing only a tarp and donated hip boots, nothing much underneath. Since childhood, not even her *hus*bands had ever seen her bare-faced. Our gorgeous hard-drinking Diana—compared for life to that poorer local farm-gal, the unbeatable good sport Ava Gardner—our same Diana now stood, sans jewelry, minus a dot or dash of lipstick and eye paint, erased nearly unrecognizable. Poor thing looked like one wet cockatiel. We made room for her on the cot and passed her a spare blanket. "It is not yet bourbon time? Mitch found me in a tree," she kept trying to sound chipper but mixed up her next: "Was up the paddle without a creek."

Then she looked at us. Di saw we knew what she meant and she need not give a do-over. We were all the same age. Diana fell to sleep almost at once. And my dear Janet, who loathes all divas, was too in shock to even properly gloat.

ENCOUNTERING YOUR NEIGHBORS in this overlit gym felt like a class reunion convened in some lesser circle of prison Hell. Even the National Guard's hanging lamps had all been caged like convicts.

You hugged your most casual friends, and why? because they'd also survived. (Some of us had not. Two pals we'd known for life had been electrocuted by a falling power line; one beloved married pair drowned inside their own new sports car during a botched dash north that washed them straight off Mill Road's dam.)

Now greeting chums, finding them unhurt, you need not say a word. You knew that their "good stuff" must be, like your heirlooms, so much soggy pulp. —Jan and I slouched here with the crowd we usually saw only at the club near month's end when you needed to eat a little of the food you'll pay for anyway.

ALL THAT MATTERED was our knowing others and being recognized by them. Broke, fresh out of shelter, we had so little else to recommend us. We *were* our aging faces. Credit lines? Our former looks. Others' memory of which beautiful house had been our own. But tonight made for a wonderful once-in-a-lifetime bond. Revival meeting. It felt either like the end of something, or a radical fresh start.

Sat feeling glad that poor Red Mabry had not heard certain flood sounds: the way many of our six hundred paired River Road maples, once robbed of supporting soil, fell into and against each other. The sound? If bowling pins were big as dinosaurs. Trees then pressed by current toward the first farm, the next town.

JUST ONE STRETCH of this armory's baseboard heat *re*ally worked; I counted twenty wide-open family Bibles spread there on gym floor-

ing, toasting some. Damp Good Books were attended by people waiting for those to slowly dry. As if stirring little campfires, seated folks
would idly reach down and flip from the crisper Old to a wetter
New Testament. I heard certain guardians muttering to themselves.
I slowly understood these sounds were not just shocked complaints
but stubborn busted prayers.

Bibles seemed more valuable for their crocheted cross-shaped
bookmarks, browned Palm Sunday fronds. Some showed handwritten names and birth dates, marriages then death dates. Books, black
and white, attended by people white and black, being dried face-up
wide-open as if meant to breathe.

Hard to describe why that first evening should seem one of the
most joyful of my life. Or maybe "memorable," which is joy at its
most attention-getting. Had I, as a house-proud man with a retired
insurance-office income, been secretly waiting for higher-octane trouble? For some outside woe past my being built around a heart this bad?

The second night would prove the killer.

And don't even mention Night #3.

Those of us who'd stayed in Falls now had no place TO stay.

Jan's first impulse was borrowing a cell phone, calling our far-
flung kids to reassure, "You didn't even *know*? It's not on the national
news yet? Well, but we're okay, thanks. The house? likely a dead-
loss but your dad and I aren't. What? Oh, honey, I will. Your dad's
waving his love as usual. Just didn't want you worried sick—and here
you had no idea!"

Emotion never behaves. Like mercury, that particular material is seriously hard to grasp. Its mass keeps turning into beads,
then vice versa. Example: The day my son graduated from Haverford, I should have felt ecstatic. "With special distinction," the dean
announced. But traces of my dad's (and *his* dad's) cardiac condition
had long since been found in our Bill #IV, passed on to him via
me. Meds were part of his life, too. Why did three sick generations'
sadness find me that one dressed-up day? Fact is, I felt so guilty for
having passed my boy such a plug heart, I honestly considered sui-

cide. A rifle in the garage seemed the least "botheration" to Janet's antiques and rugs. So why was this flood night unlike any other? This night of the day when I lost our house and cars and her great-great-grandfolks' only oil portraits, why should an unaccountable elation now come to call?

Maybe because, being like everybody else, I felt briefly washed of guilt. I could claim God's love or be another hard luck case or both, whichever suited me. I need no longer actually succeed. Not like those that fled Falls early to strain for stardom elsewhere. I was Bill Mabry, formerly of The River Road, which was presently The River.

Maybe I had suddenly floated into my own fated Phase *II*?

Somebody announced our dinner tonight would be hot dogs, meant for the grammar school now closed, either with or without buns.

SINCE EVEN NOW our part of the world is still farmed, most of us keep big deep freezes. Janet and I had shucked, then "put up" this past summer's exceptional Silver Queen corn grown on her family's last country holding. Like Doc's duck specimen freezer, other neighbors' were stocked with game, but theirs proved edible. Everybody specializes in a different delicacy.

The Blanchards have a summer place in Maine and so they always fly home south with August's lobsters onboard. Everybody stashes shrimp we peeled ourselves, quail we've plucked, and all of it was suddenly left unrefrigerated. We knew we'd have no electricity hereabouts for weeks, at least. Easily a million bucks' worth of our neighbors' best possible food was now going going gone.

Timothy and Tomothy Bixby got suddenly inspired. Being teens they were insisting on being called "Thomas" and "Timothy." But nobody could give up that other, it was such fun to say. They'd become famous when Doc Roper breathed them both back to life. (Later rumors claimed that all along they'd been secretly Roper's sons! Not true.) Twins were slated for full-ride swim team scholarships at the University of Miami.

We heard how, as the Bixbys' pool emptied into their sodden

house, boys had already wrestled their mom's butane gas grill up into their red pickup's bed. Boys set all good stuff from their own family-freezer over a slow flame—venison, homemade sausage, lump-crab picked by many a loud Bixby watching UNC basketball on River-side's first giant screen.

While one twin kept the grill lit in the truck's bed, the other (practically-amphibious for life) launched their outboard. He sped off to fetch the best from others' room-temp freezers. We River Road-ers all knew, as by internal pirate map, where the finest of everything edible must be thawing. We also guessed if that house stood on red clay high enough to not yet be submerged.

Approached by a Bixby, folks were delighted to see their perish-ables used. Being largely Scotch-Irish, we do hate waste. (Fact is, the richer the Scots, the more the squandering of leftovers is hated, the more Scots salt away to become their future generations' sometimes-wasteful wealth.) Twins made this food bank seem a game. Didn't much matter *who* was eating your cache, so long as it got utilized, maybe enjoyed.

The Bixbys, though famously, almost identically, handsome, were hardly chefs. But tonight's ingredients proved of such high quality, something extra happened. All that okra and halibut. Tuna steaks. Pheasant breasts, white sea scallops tender as baby bottoms, mahi-mahi caught from charter-boats way way out. By the time twins pulled their truck through armory's double doors, you could already smell their brew on glorious slow boil. Dogs were trying to get in. The scent, it traveled like a song. It was the smell of B.C.

Boys stood hand-casting spices into one huge bubbling pot: bay leaves, cayenne. I'd call their game-muddle pure *Male* food. No pars-ley sprigs, no candlelit "presentation," as Jan's lately been calling it. No, you've got your one pooled substance, available tonight only. Into this one load, a man puts everything he means and is. How good did it taste? You had to have been there.

Since regular utensils were mostly underwater, kids stirred their brew with one aluminum canoe-oar. We were already lined up, about to eat the dry hot dogs provided. We'd felt glad enough for those! Now here came Timothy-Tomothy, brown as Seminoles, wearing flip-flops, cut-off jeans. Beautiful hellions from birth, they appeared a platoon about six-strong, not just two kids on some frat-house lark. I watched food-serving twins move as one unit and marveled how that must feel. To still be sleek with health, with hearts the size of such torsos, shoulders. Imagine having a man-friend so close, this efficient and forever within reach.

There was a certain married white lady who, a few years back, had baptized Tomothy-Timothy into sexual practice. She looked significantly older now while the twins looked somehow even younger. She was here tonight and hungry as the rest of us. Her traveling husband, now queued behind her, was among the few Riversiders present unaware of her history. She came tentatively forward, for food. Both Bixbys grinned down at her. Tomothy said, "For you and your man, a double portion, ma'am. Mighty good neighbors you've been." All she said back was, "No problem." Her husband, an explainer, then explained to her and everyone nearby, "Outstanding youngsters, these. Enterprising."

All of us, the poor and the loaded, wearing every nasty kind of housedress or running-outfit, we sure lined up quick beside the Bixbys' red Dodge truck. We stood obedient as orphans, holding our paper plates. Odd, I kept thinking of my dad's "town" grave, underwater, a shock for him.

I noticed certain Republicans, one I'd heard rail for years against any person who'd ever take a single handout. I saw how they kept edging themselves and each other toward the line's front. I seemed to see the comedy of things with fresh eyes. I seemed to have forgotten something that dulled me, held me back.

We soon retreated to our cots. We sat there eating. Best stuff you ever put into your mouth. Sitting in a room this big, it tasted far better for being absolutely everybody's. If this was a leveling, it had a fine collective flavor. I'd taken no meds in six hours but felt so avid, clear.

That first long night, we talked. We went back for Bixby seconds, thirds. We just ate and cried and ate.

3

I'D EXITED MY sixties, feeling over-aware of Dad's dying mid-swing at age fifty-one. I had come to despise the worries of keeping up a big old riverside house. It'd been Red's great wish for himself, meaning me.

Its water's-edge window screens kept rusting lacy, kept making you appear a failure. I'd been warned against any further heavy lifting. Hence the pointless expense of hiring high-school kids who might show up and mow and edge your acre and a half even twice a month at any price.

Yes, our stone house at river's edge was kind of a museum to scenes of former family good times. Lately it'd served mainly as the ideal setting for her heirloom furniture. Country-made Chippendale, first threatened by Sherman's torches; now global-warming's wet! No fair!

And yet, with this much standing water, no longer would I have to micromanage some place our kids required three days each Christmas. I'd never again slice myself while fixing the danged lawn mower. (See, I believed my own lies about home owner's hardship.) Sitting on an army cot, I had at last become a "portable unit" after a lifetime hooked to one thick black extension cord. I was no longer a risk-averse insurance salesman to whom nothing had ever happened. True, now I more or less *had* nothing. Except of course some money in the bank. But tonight that eventual unknown amount seemed quite abstract, dry ice. I imagined I had nothing past the not-uninteresting story of losing it all! Surely there was a lesson floating in here somewhere: I again felt poor as that kid in a Myrtle Beach cowboy shirt, proud of his ducktail, the mullet of its day.

With our exceptional armory meal now eaten, somebody produced his old college sterling flask. Jack Daniel's is some invention. Slow burn, it topped off that stew just right. Slumped back on "our" cots, we lounged here, passing its proofing around. Though inwardly hysterical, post-traumatic whatever-ed, we flask-passing husbands and wives somehow briefly felt like smart teenagers during their first long unchaperoned night as camp counselors.

Was only then a tennis partner said, "Bill, is it true what they're saying about poor Roper?"

I FIGURED DOC'S had been washed out like everybody along The River Road. (Fact is I'd forgotten Roper these past few hours, kind of an unusual and secret freshening relief.) Our friend told how Doc and Marge had lost their house and everything, naturally, like the rest. But, maybe worse than forfeiting home and cars, Doc's wide bay windows overlooking the river?—those 20-foot studio windows honeycombed with shelving to display his decade and more of Marion masterpieces?—well, they'd busted out early. Popping loose, those lifted free, then sort of rafted off a ways. The glass had been found intact out past the Halseys' diving raft. But all his masterful ducks?

It seemed that even before the Ropers' ground floor got soaked, Doc's waterside studio, river-view on three sides, had been crushed, gutted. Once Doc and Marge were roused by the young spaniels' barking, Roper dived off their second-story roof, swam out there wearing pajama bottoms. Apart from a newly-started decoy still clamped fast in his worktable vise, all two hundred of his finest saved-back waterbirds, they'd floated free.

Doc's life's work—Phase *Two* of it, I mean—cleanly gone missing. But wouldn't the corps of his work turn up once the all-clear signal sounded? Wouldn't scattered ducks form a flotilla and someway swim home to Doc? To dock!

His freezer full of dead creatures had also been bounced around by wild currents, wrestled to one side, then busted open like a coffin. Now even Roper's frozen specimen birds were swimming free again.

———

"WHAT A SHAME," I finally said, sounding insincere even to myself. "But let's us try and keep it in perspective? Before, we heard how the Blanchards' granddaughter wandered into their half-basement looking for their cat (which is likely still on top of our fridge) and somehow fell, then almost drowned down there before they heard her. The Eddie McCombs made a run for high ground in their new T-bird, got swept off Mill Road's bridge. I guess Hackney and Betty Eatman were found in their bed still wearing their eye masks and earplugs. And everybody we know has become 'a Homeless' in two hours. And yet, even so, like me, you're all still hung up on how Roper's lost some wood painted to seem . . . to be . . . uh? ducks? Why do we always put him first? Ya'll notice that? Even tonight. Will we ever get over his stitching us up? That was his *job*. I may be tipsy from Tad's flask, but sometimes (and I think Janet'll back me up in this) I believe . . . *Doc* is a decoy! He *looks* like us other ducks. But his paint's a bit bright. Man hasn't moved around much lately, has he? Why's he always s'perfect? Why will we forgive him anything?"

Janet said, "Bill."

But I finished, "And yet, too, I am, I'm basically so *sad* for him. Complicated, I guess. Sorry. Amazing person, of course. Everybody loves him to pieces. Me, too, so much, God knows. But with all this other happening, it's . . . it's just . . ."

Others swapped looks but most gave immediate nods. Sure, I'd overstated. Sure, somehow my own self-pity always included Doc. But my other thoughts could not be news to anybody present. Janet flashed me her familiar *You've really gone too far again* look. And I felt that, sure.

—Look, is it possible we truly secretly hate the best our flock can offer? Why was I so daily interested then pissed at him? Because of Roper's underrating me? Hadn't he kept me alive? Did I resent his ceasing to "treat" me just as my left side's numbing got worse? Did I blame Doc's losing faith in my own boyish "potential" as I shot past seventy?

And what did I expect he'd think I might someday *do*? Why

had I, the man best seen from afar if at all, chosen as my closest friend the best-loved man in town? The very guy who'd need
buddyhood least! Some secret wish to live in permanent check-
mate? Why'd he refuse to let me own his best carved beauty? I half-
imagined it, under my arm, essential flood-luggage tonight. Funny,
but just then I decided that the two of us, Doc and I, are a lot alike,
especially when alone! Twins, nearly. But, as soon as anybody's solitude is interrupted, see . . . ? I'd never solve that data-collecting
quality-control problem. But tonight, one mystery resolved itself.
I'd always wondered why Doc, sixth in his Yale class, chose to come
on back to Falls and stay. Now I understood: It'd been his one best
way to be alone. Here he was a "doc" for us before med school,
already a given. He could leave us with that most attractive replica.
It let Roper live as solitary as I felt. Still, any bird's-eye view of his
rounds would've shown you a man mobbed.

So, why had I been waking all these years to have my coffee on
our deck, just to sort of note where all the Roper cars had parked last
night before I could even feel *awake*? Why did I hope he'd make one
last dawn river-swim? *Why?* I always felt that I was missing something. Who'd tell me?

STRANGE, BUT, HEARING about his losses, first thing that came
was sadness Roper'd never invited me back into his precious inner
sanctum. Ruined now. He might've shown me everything he made,
even before he did the others. Second, I felt some odd relief at the
end of "Marion's" art. A menacing emotion, one I'm not real proud
of. Recovering some scrap of my dignity, I did finally tell our half-
drunk crowd, "At least the carvings he sold *out* of town will still
show all he could do. And, hey, come to think of it, if Doc had
let me buy that wood duck (his best single work, though he never
seemed to know) and if I had just put that in the showcase on our
third floor . . ."

"It'd be Gone with the Wind *like the rest of everything us Riversiders
ever owned, fool!*" So one tennis partner snapped.

I laughed, "Yeah, well. Point taken . . ."

OF COURSE, WE still had Janet's empty-nesters' cockatiels, birds that irritated me so much I was ready to make stuffed ducks of *them*.

At ten p.m. that first public night of many, officials had doused our armory's overhead lamps. Some people switched on hoarded little flashlights. The only other brightness came from near the bathrooms or out in the ugly khaki foyer. Not five minutes in, one small dog yelped, I could tell, crying in its sleep. Some omen: Yorkies having nightmares on Night #1. Water still rising, and personnel seeing things.

I fought to doze in that giant room full of snoring men. (How had their wives not long ago *shot* them, us?) Between our cots, near the birds' covered cage and her laptop, I held Janet's hand. She'd conked out at once, though Jan ("Didn't catch a wink") would deny it all tomorrow.

To ease toward any drifting scrap of sleep, I found myself mentally collecting poor Roper's scattered birds. It became a mission that only some close friend might undertake. Like colored rosary beads— two hundred or more of our pal's very best were out now, unparoled; released down forks of ditches, they kept somehow spreading into rivers that eventually crosshatched deltas become one raw ocean. Till last night, each bird had been worth thousands. I imagined them already exiting our state on whirlpooled currents, some sucked down into gasping sewers. While I kept trying to sleep, a map assembled above my cot. Like those old manhunt charts you see in police movies, grease-penciled within narrowing circles, sectors, "where suspect last seen."

MY BLOOD THINNERS, various meds, had last been spied at home, set neatly along one raftlike bedside table. Pill bottles now riding this same duck-water.

"That's mighty rough," I'd said to friends. "Roper had so much *work* in those. But, hey, he can make others. The sec this is over, we'll all start again. And so will 'Marion,' unsinkable . . ."

But, lying here beneath an itchy army blanket, one hand in my wife's hand, the other curled behind my head, I knew better: I was already somehow aging up pretty good myself. Doc had stumbled headlong up into his eighties, right? Even at my age, given my condition, I knew true resiliency requires serious health, pretty solid ground to stand on.

Pretending I would sleep, I guessed I'd really only rest. Kept recalling news of Roper's achievements throughout school, even with me trailing ten years behind him. Every club you joined he had either founded or presided over. Some groups never even bothered with an election his year. Cincinnatus. Others forced the man to lead. There was some quality. Not just his looks or style, whatever. Did I *want* it? Was *that* it? Or maybe I hoped to grow more *like* him, even now? He meant so much to me, I just didn't yet know why.

He might find energy to rebuild their house. Might even design a new place for Marge and him on slightly higher ground. But to re-create that unexpected bonus round he'd carved from his last decade? that was going to be a long shot. Restarting Phase II a second time, at eighty-two? Tough for anybody.

Even for a Doc.

AROUND ME, WHISPERERS still catalogued who'd been saved, who not. Which veterinary hospital had gone under, killing our beloved pets hidden exactly there for safety's sake. And which geniuses among us actually owned flood insurance? Three households! One, Mitch's, the other Riverside insurance agent of choice; the second Janet's and mine. A third, one river-edge pennywise widow-dowager-client of mine who'd signed up over objections. All of us, we would keep quiet about the embarrassment of having stayed put while also keeping ourselves "covered."

I felt myself struggling to relax while on the brink of some finding: I'd been recognized by neighbors with embraces I could feel were truly meant. That finally convinced me. All along, I'd been a major part of Riverside. Safe in that at last. But *why?*

Because it was all gone now.

Somehow, tired unto death, I muttered that: "It's gone now, it's gone now, it's . . ." and slept like some dim if trusting child.

Gosh, I missed my father.

4

I WOKE DECIDING we were having an adventure. Mr. Safari had come for us. Our kids once made me re-re-read *Peter Pan in Kensington Gardens* aloud to them night after night. We loved the flying part but I made them stay grounded in beds at least till reading ended. That darn Peter had been a genius; he knew to stop growing on the non-shaving side of puberty. He could look over into adulthood's promised land but he preferred not to take that bait. And this morning I recalled the flying boy's simple line, "Dying would be an awfully big adventure."

A thanks-and-recovery service was announced for noon that day at All Saints Episcopal. *Thanks* seemed misplaced, *recovery* impossible, but we went. The one FEMA woman said she couldn't let us stay in the armory all morning, said they'd need to sweep up, empty our trash cans.

The old brick sanctuary Dad had loved still stood downtown, on fairly high ground. The donors, 1820s Paxtons, must've seen to this before our town maples obscured Falls' highs and lows. I'd heard that First Presbyterian and its graveyard were submerged knee-deep. There was a borrowed cabin cruiser tied to a handy basketball goal. Old friends, minus the Ropers, all piled in. Somebody said this beautiful boat had once belonged to Doc Dennis S—.

As a boy, I used to dream of flying. With your hometown drowned, you move over it, as if both underwater and at angel's height. The smells come as surprises, too. We passed the chimney of our best African-American beauty salon; adjoining water wore a bubble roof of shampoo. Air grew sweet with all that coconutty lost cologne. I wanted to swing back for a second sniff but our friend's inboard soon chewed into an ill-placed treetop. We just clambered out onto a loading dock then waded-walked the rest of the way.

Somehow we three couples went from moaning to giggling over nothing, like kids, not a worry in the world. The full sun was out as if to show us more perfectly everything lost. Our deck shoes kept making comical Little Rascals squishy sounds. I felt stunned to where, if any of my male tennis partners had taken my free hand (like how kindergarten boys wander around), I would have enjoyed that. All rules gone. Most. A good-sized catfish made a U-turn at the corner of Church Street and Main. With that there came this streaming sense of a new chance. Another life, elsewhere. But walking in water proves harder than that same action in air. I had to slow down, stop at intervals . . . catching . . . breath. Others indulged me, circling back, then trudging but at my pace.

Marge Roper stood in our church's forecourt, already running interference. She explained that everything was fine, though Doc was not himself quite yet. Everybody guessed his loss must feel particularly bitter. You can buy new TVs, etc., but your own art hand-carved . . . ? Odd, today I remembered wondering why this man had not—given his amazing skill—carved small people, instead. They surely outrank everything. Me, now, if I could sculpt or write, as a subject, only people would interest me. Why they do stuff! There'd be so much to know! But, making decoys, hadn't he just been doing further xerox copies of known imitations of what started as pure waterbirds? With human portraits, no two can ever look alike. Hell, if I could have ever been a great artist, I bet I could've been a *great* artist.

I SOON NOTED Roper standing by himself off in back. Everyone had heard, his coveted works were inhaled by deluge. And we'd turned up just as somebody brought one of his lost decoys back to him. The gal had found it, floating, head forward, right-side up.

She hand-delivered it straight to this service, guessing Doc might be here. The young woman served cocktails out at the Starlite and maybe on Fridays "danced." After her mother's cancer, the family was said to still owe Roper huge back-bills. Delighted, she turned up in her full barmaid war paint. Hadn't the young doc once swapped service? Well, she'd fished this relic from a ditch near her trailer seven miles from Riverside. Had it wrapped up special in a Hardee's burger bag! Gal must've felt in an amazing position to now barter down those thousands overdue. She did not ask aloud how much this art was worth to him; but you saw that question buckling her tender made-up face. "Bless you," Marge said, simple. As if human thanks were all the payment needed. The poor girl blinked. But, even if disappointed herself, she lingered, expecting it would cheer *him*.

This cedar teal had drifted through some spilled barn-red enamel. One whole wing's paint flapped free like burned human skin. Contact with water had already ruined its side, though the ably-carved neck and head remained unwarped. The finder, meaning well, now handed this duck to Roper right here before the church for all to see. Unpaid, she'd still waited for the smile, his recovery. If Marge wondered how exactly to stop this happening, she maybe felt too drained to intervene.

DOC SIMPLY HELD the thing. He looked down at it resting in both his hands. Roper's blue-white eyes were fixed right on it. And yet Doc acted as if he'd never seen a duck before, much less a carved one, much less the odd concept of a "decoy" meant to fake out a real one as one of its own kind.

Made a fairly sorry sight. Seeing Roper at a loss, Julia Abernethy and several other former lady-patients "tuned up" pretty good. I stared at the awkward way he clutched the object. Later, during service, I'd note how Doc absently gripped it as some child might—by the head— fist around its neck. You sensed he was anywhere but in our shared present tense. I watched him so. One word came to me: "adrift."

Doc stared ahead as if awaiting some signal or alarm from right in back of him. Not much paint was really left on the recovered carv-

ing. That let me know. Floodwater must be highly acidic, petrochem-
icaled, so much hog waste. It would prove terribly toxic to us all. Just
twelve hours in water had burned paint off his carving, the equivalent of an hour's belt-sanding.

Already, I think, we knew. It wasn't just the water's doings that
seemed bad. Water itself was.

STRANGE THING ABOUT people old as us. Some get visibly rickety for a while, then they'll briefly heal right up on you. Others look
youthful forever till, after catching one cold, after your not seeing
them for three weeks, they turn up at Les Wilkins's pool party. And
you must ask your host, "Who is that shaky *old* one on the end?"

"Why, that's Emmie, silly. You-all were in Miss Thorp's third
grade together. Your *eyes* are failing."

"Something round here's falling apart, boy-o. —Ain't just my eyes."
Was like that now with Roper.

During service, as the German organ's Bach processional sounded
particularly sad because especially perfect, Roper leaned forward,
spine clear off the pew. He stared, fixed, ahead. Doc seemed to have
forgotten the liturgy he'd had by heart since age three. (Selfish, I
couldn't help hope he'd remember a long-range plan he'd mapped out
once to keep my sad-sack heart at click.)

When others, exiting, spoke his way, Doc did try, did nod. Did
fight to *seem* polite. But that in itself looked unlike him, his acting just
dutiful. Roper squinted as at strangers. He still cradled that peeling
bird the way some college running back will nurse the pigskin in the
crook of his right arm. Odd, but behind Doc, a stained-glass Madonna
held her bandaged babe in the same darn cradling pose.

I could tell that Roper hadn't wanted to come. Probably dreaded
facing sympathy, a crowd. But Marge, usually fairly agreeable-acting,
had likely forced him. Hoping his being near familiars might jolt
Doc back toward normal. He must've begged to keep away from
church, while hiding where? They had no above-water home or car.
The guy suddenly looked like someone scared to be left alone.

This past master at teasing people, at remembering our exact lipid-triffid totals—today failed to start or hold one conversation. I briefly tried. "Got to be mighty upsetting . . ." was my own brilliant start. But Marge cut me one sad look, no-go. Doc blinked. I knew she was right. I shut up but it hurt me that I, of all folks, had just failed to make true contact. Given what I had to mean to him, this stupid blurt of mine would just slay me later.

After service, in the crowd, he attempted answering others but only if Marge forced him: "They're *talk*ing to you, honey. You see Whit and Cora here."

"Cora," he nodded. "Cora, how's your bad athlete's foot?"

Cora, slowed, said, "Better," but looked away. Never before had Doc revealed one office secret aloud. Cora here had just lost her house, family photos, bull terrier and cars. Itchy feet—the least of her problems.

We all noted how Margie stared at Doc—now an ancient-looking white man stuck vulnerable out in midday glare. He as yet stood carrying one wooden duck by its neck; the thing hung at his side with no more care than a commuter offers the usual battered briefcase.

Not him! people said. Of all our unlikeliest strong ones, don't let it be our Doc unravels all at once.

Sure he'd just lost his handiwork. But what else personal had drifted off with Marion's copyrighted aquatic birds? Hadn't Doc carved those things *to* float? Hadn't he weighted their chests with molten lead he then painted over? Surely he'd intended their superb balance, sailboat poise. Doc's cedar exemplars had proved so stream-lined they hadn't simply sunk in his backyard, had they? There he might've retrieved them, saved the paint. But, no, his proved far too lifelike. Doc's birds, painted bold as little flags, rode sudden currents perfectly; become real emblems of American freedom. Born indoors, they'd gone off in search of true wilderness. They *took* to it. Like, well . . . like what they were. Or at least so perfectly resembled.

Their very excellence scattered Doc's the fastest!

WE'D ALREADY HEARD how at dawn yesterday he paid big money, hiring a speedboat from one of Tomothy's friends. We guessed this vessel should've been out saving people, right? But Roper'd commandeered it. The Bixby kids did owe him a favor, big time. Doc had ordered wide sweeps to track his waterfowl. No luck. Disobedient creations, creatures! To risk sounding biblical a sec: having tasted of the water of the knowledge of good and evil, they left home and Roper fast.

I could already fancy them, spread out like some little floating Chaplin-tramps bobbing on stray trenches along farm roads, working their way at twenty-feet-an-hour up woodland creeks. A few by now must probably be a hundred miles of standing-water away, rocking clear out on the chill Atlantic.

EASY TO SAY his were only "fakes," hacked from wood then enameled. Being all thumbs myself (including the one with stitch marks in it), I knew his task's great difficulty. I sensed how rare was the quiet talent for making what appeared literally wild. (His birds never looked farm-raised; instead Roper's were visibly little scrappers, criminal renegades living by their strengths in the unfair open.)

You might say: people who love something too much, live at greater risk. And yet, that's bound to be the one sane way forward. Surely our determination to never lose what we've made to love, that, in itself, means an early sort of decoy death.

I'd seen our house go under. Naturally, I missed it. All afternoon, while wandering the reopened armory, I kept patting my pockets for keys (now underwater). I hated how our kids couldn't now come home and stay upstairs in rooms full of their Little League trophies and the complete Nancy Drew. They'd never rewalk literal ground where they first crawled then stepped then struggled upward to battle one another. I found I even missed their little squabbles. An only child myself, I always loved the role of referee.

I mostly fancied sunset light in the northwest corner of our foyer, thrown against old willow-bough wallpaper through bubbled glass at six o'clock on winter afternoons. That picture hit me with a daily pang like lost love. It was, I guess.

And yet, unlike Doc with all his powers to forfeit, I was left feeling, if admittedly poorer, about a decade younger. Now I got a clearer picture of my first house, before Paxton's oddball legacy to Red. It had been set up on four unsteady-looking piles of bricks, the simple white of a country box. Our lawn grew tobacco. We had, not a river stealing around behind, but one whole honest horizon that stayed put.

Having lost our place on The River Road, I felt shaken simpler. I did feel lighter-weight. Poor, I felt adventurous.

5

SIX MONTHS AFTER the flood a few locals still believed it: believed they could simply dry out their old homes, soon move back in. Seemed as logical as most painful delusions.

Already four pulmonary deaths among our crowd: all the heaviest smokers went that quick. Especially those two-packers-a-day who'd insisted on then going home to dig up their better inherited peony bushes. Peonies can live over sixty years. Our coughing diggers breathed in all that fresh shovel-loosened filth. And, after the pain of home-delivered oxygen tanks, four amiable locals died that first half-year A.D. —After Deluge.

The minute we'd seen maple-syrup-brown liquid burglarize our homes, most of us had known. No going back. Hadn't we decoded the ruined paint on Doc's first recovered decoy? Old folks now, we, like him, lived symptomatically. He had been the first to send a dove across the flood, a test case to see if, finding no land, it might not return safe. It came back okay but immediately blistered. It had not made him hopeful that his bird looked soaked in kerosene, then red paint, with a final wash of hog-piss battery acid.

Receded water left a scummy chalk, pink-brown across our every twig and doorknob. It was a dangerous-looking color, right out of our 1950s science fiction films.

There's a Bible line about rendering unto Caesar what is Caesar's, and unto God, God's. Riverside's new variation ran, "When in doubt, side with the River. Render unto River whatever's River's."

Which *was*?

Everything except our wits.

Everything except our dry ole dry-martini lives, thank God!

WE COULD ALL list our treasures lost. We agreed about what had been most valuable moneywise: Les Wilkins's two-million-dollar antique car collection, stored in the lately-Chapter-Elevened Wilkins Tobacco Auction Warehouse.

Poor Les had sunk many an inherited penny into his two 1937 Cord Phaeton convertibles, a squadron of early Bentleys and Jags, plus, best, the 1928 Hispano-Suiza touring car elaborate as its maker's name. It had been all beaten silver and lacquered burgundy, commissioned by Gloria Swanson. Streamlined, fitted inside with blond-wood carving, it'd always seemed more a ship than any auto. Its silver horn played a song about blowing bubbles. All submerged in four minutes. Asked how he felt, Les answered for months after, "Flat tire, flat tire."

His wife finally admitted she'd had to keep Les restrained those first ten days. She'd locked him in their borrowed home's attic sewing room. Poor guy kept wanting to swim underwater in order to simply sit behind the wheel of Swanson's sunken Hispano-Suisa and sound its silver trumpets and end his life down there, in style.

Also gone to mud: Julia Abernethy's real Degas drawing, a beautiful racehorse one. Raleigh's art museum had been after it for decades but you know how close-fisted most Abernethys are.

Still, we all concurred about the loss that stirred us most. Unlike Les's Hollywood town cars or Julia's French pastel, this was the one lost masterwork made *here*. Carved by someone who'd stayed, and

likewise meant his creations to. He'd chosen birds he knew as peculiar to our region. —A fleet now scattered to the Seven Seas.

At our Recovery Talent Show, everybody's favorite gossipy oph-
thalmologist brought down the house playing a borrowed banjo as
he hound-dogged:

> *I left a million five and change,*
> *Down by the river-side,*
> *Down by . . .*

Four full-tilt divorces had been well and nastily in progress. Then
water rose many feet. And, once these bickering folks, the parents
of assorted pretty semi-disappointing children, spent hours pulling
each other through a million gallons of sewage, by the time they were
found high up the Blanchards' water oak, they appeared to be French-
kissing. They proved so wet if fused, it was hard to get the lovebirds
separately saved!

They'd never split now. They would only fight like beasts of
burden for the right to carry one another forward; out of this world
into whatever if any adventure's coming next. A childhood sweetheart rededicated herself to her first husband, after having com-
mitted five children and one half-century to another, some Yankee.
"And you, my lifelong friends, whyn't you *tell* me? —Tony never
friggin *got* Falls."

Certain other marriages, from their wedding days forth, had been
called "disasters waiting to happen." Now one had. Would it make
these shipwreck unions seem better or worse? We'd best wait and see.
What *else* had we to do?

Our gang lived uneasily reestablished in an over-new development. "Hilltop" is no more a hill than Falls is a waterfall. But this
clay tract rises a scant two feet above-sea-level, much higher than
dear sunken Riverside. Cotton grew here and so our newly planted
grass still shows plowings' crenellations.

Our homes up here they're all smaller-blander than the grand half-timbered barns we once filled with kids and junk. Prestige? a goner. Disaster claimed our antiquities and made us finally efficient! We sacrificed elbow-room but spared ourselves five daily huffing ascents toward a second story, only to forget why we climbed. Our crowd was sixty to ninety now; the river had done editorial home-downsizing *for* us.

Finally, we all now lived "maintenance included." No need for hiring daily maids, weekly yardmen. Free at last! I will never touch another lawn mower.

Age has its privileges.

6

THE MARION ROPERS bought into Hilltop last. They took that smallish skylighted unit at our block's far end. Post-flood, us refugee Riversiders tended to party hardier. Frantic weeknight dance things. We played Benny Goodman, James Brown, Sarah Vaughan, the Beatles. Anything. No, anything but rap. Somebody's kid had given them discs. "No rap!" Diana de Pres cried. "After what we've been through?" Our crowd certainly drank more, or maybe just more openly. "Like fish," was one flood joke now out of favor, overused.

"How you feeling? You look washed-out." That was another line we'd long since bored of. Every English phrase and pun suddenly seemed liquid-based. Each brimmed with refreshed permission to sip bourbon. By now, why the hell *not?*

What was the bank going to do, come confiscate your Chippendale highboy, your things, your *house?* Would they punish us seniors with sledgehammers, forcing ladies to go make little rocks out of rocks big as the Broken Heart? Might they stick us into nice dry jail cells, serve us three meals a day? If so, right now might be good.

Our long cocktail blasts featured finger foods scarcely underwriting offsetting vodka and gin. Our parties grew feverish again and endless. We felt moneyed the way four-year-olds at birthday parties feel, cake and candles all the proof of luck we'd need.

Today was today and we would gobble it. Shrinks from Raleigh commuted, overbooked. IRAs, "wealth management," we had just enough put aside not to think constantly of that. Of course, there was always a worry of outlasting nest-eggs, depending on our kids, becoming bores, then nuisances. Foreign travel seemed a threat now. Venice? Water for streets? Been there, swum those. As for cruises!

I used to say things like, "So much of life comes down to our river." Well, it could all come up on you overnight like food poisoning.

Old neighbors now live within easy hearty-partying distance. —Given yards so small—true drinkers can literally crawl home. Poor Les Wilkins sometimes does. Down on all fours like a basset hound. He misses specific cars so much, he'll tell you how he got ahold of each. Like Casanova, ancient, recounting servant girls seduced. Les still lives in mourning for sixty antique autos. Odd, the fates waiting each of us. My own? To mythologize the farm-boy past of a dad who wanted all that "country" sheared off him like bad wool. To die in sight of the one off-duty doctor who might've saved you.

We seem to be returning to our old dance-card days, reliving certain engagement party blowouts of our crazed youths. Last night, Diana de Pres got sick from Brandy Alexanders and the outcome looked even less pretty than it had on her, all over her, at age sixteen.

MARGE ROPER WOULD turn up alone at a few cocktail hours but never did stay long. The few times she brought Doc he'd hover in the foyer. He would answer only direct questions, eyes averted. That brilliant gift for diagnosis—wasted scanning floor tiles, an umbrella stand.

Doc kept mainly to himself. Nothing new in that. But now he was seen taking walks. People claimed his therapist had suggested hikes might be good for him. Might give Doc something "focused" to do, mornings-evenings. Roper'd dropped a lot of weight. People said he now looked "ropy," an accurate word that contained both his curious name and new unknotting appearance.

Roper had taken to patrolling while using one tall stick he'd found. No carving on it, alas. We all wanted him to start again, even simplest whittling. Only that might be Doc's ticket to his grand delayed Phase III.

Marge said he now called such long strolls "looking" or "going out looking." Margie told my Jan that, many nights at dinner, Doc made perfect sense. For up to twenty minutes he seemed to know exactly what had happened, to be up to date. On one subject alone did he stay crazed: his life's scattered hand-work. He just knew he wanted it back. Did he see his decoys as patients wandered off, needing Doc alone? No. I wish. He wanted wood simply for being the very carved material made valuable by his once having valued it.

MY HEART, ABOUT like Dad's, had been not-good for decades, then got worse all at once. Flood-inspired adrenaline had fooled me into feeling resurrected for whole weeks. My heart's tire-patch inner-tube analogy had, for me, been overdone. Soon nothing's left *but* balloon, caulking and the stents, seals.

Dr. Gita asked me why I had not been to see her for the check-ups lately. Why had I never stayed in touch with certain Duke-UNC specialists? Hadn't Roper referred me the day I quit my Monday checkups? She told me Doc had made her vow she'd give me special care. The manila-bound notes he'd left were rubber-banded, novel-thick. And poor Gita herself, hadn't she mailed me a handwritten note, reminding me, remember? But I'd been avoiding her, had I not?

I scratched my head, imitating a former internist. "Well, ma'am, once Doc retired, guess I sort of forgot."

"Yes. I am hearing a great deal of that, William. Never have met so many thought he worked for them alone. You've at least let me keep your prescriptions going. But I'm afraid that, by putting off all appointments this year and a half since the flood—I must be very

clear here—you've lost a good bit more function. You're understand-
ing me? At least nod, please." So I did, nod.

FOUND I DIDN'T much care either way. Found the flood had sucked
back every bit of quickening that'd first rafted me through it. That
energy got reneged plus a surcharge for its use. Found I couldn't do
all that many "activities" per day anymore. One, tops.

Janet begged me not to drive. But without a car I'd be one dead
duck truly finished. I told her, if I felt Doc's predicted "flutter before
implosion" I'd hit the blinkers, pull over pretty darn quick. She
always swore I was being selfish. Said I was bound to kill "some fine
young family." Jan feared I'd take out a worthy attractive couple and
their several kids. I knew she was only remembering us. Our Volvo
station wagon (not unlike the Ropers') had once been a mess of car
seats, bottle-warmers plugged into our dashboard lighter, pink kitty
toys spongy underfoot. Jan had made me, an old man, into the enemy
of Family Promise. Or maybe Time had.

Post-flood, remembering my own father's end, I gave up even
hanging near the links. The club bar has always been called Hole
Nineteen. That phrase took on a grave-side clifflike edge for me.
Hell, I'd lately been forced to finally give up even morning decaf! My
quality of life? Of *what*?

I moped around these new-built eleven hundred square feet.

I realized that, for my last four years in the old place B.C., I had
been taking daily naps, in Jill's . . . in my daughter's girlhood room.
Every frilly hand-drawn thing in there I noted, kept just in its place.
I wrote notes and paid bills in Lottie's office. Small spaces I liked
best. Less chance of misplacing things with all pertinent objects at
hand, in view.

Now I wished for a stellar late-life hobby, *very* late. I kept mainly
watching our animal shows on PBS, rereading WWII, trying not to
drive my poor patient Janet mad by my driving too often. But if she
visited neighbors or got a long-enough phone-call, I would snitch the
car keys. Couldn't help it. After the flood she'd refused to buy me a

replacement car. Claimed she could better monitor the one. Escaped,
I often drove downhill into our old neighborhood, roads cracked but
familiar. Most toxic houses had been razed per health department
orders.

ABOUT THEN, MAYBE a year and a half post-flood, you'd sometimes
see Doc walking far off the interstate. Raleigh now sent its traffic and
four-lanes clear out Falls' way. Farm lanes from my boyhood muscled
up with off-ramps.

Roper might be near the concrete drainage-trench under some
busy cloverleaf. Down there, alongside roadkill beagles, cement's
graffiti, bent grocery carts, you'd spy his windblown head. It'd once
been the preferred hood ornament of Davidson, then Yale, that head-
ful of local life-saving was lost to use, to us. To me. His best friend.

He'd be striding along depending on his guide-stick. You'd see
Roper poking through piles of drifted leaves. He'd move along, over-
turning garbage, always alone, prodding, on the stalk for something. My Janet had spotted him wandered way out past Red Oak
Grange. Doc was poling himself along a roadside gully, his tennis-
shoes resembling cinder blocks of mud. She told how he dragged forward, head-down, scanning the way certain poorer folks hereabouts
once hunted Coke bottles for selling back to stores.

Surely he was seeking one of his Manhattan-worthy artworks. Or
was he looking for one real live duck, to be a new model, to inspire
him? The sight of Roper's quest felt so sad it grew half-sickening.
He'd never been one to sit still.

You reach an age when you open your morning newspapers not
to Sports, the Funnies, but Obits. At our age, Jan and I knew dozens
who had "preceded us," as morticians must say. Such acquaintances
became your own silent majority of friends. But it wasn't that. That
in itself is strangely not so tough on people of our given vintage. It's
not the lost; it's the lingerers that slay you! You don't usually have to
see the deceased up and out *walk*ing.

With him in motion, Doc's white hair now looked rat-nest fly-away as Einstein's. White eyebrows, once sleek as otter fur, now coiled with stray white hairs overshooting everywhichaway. Try as Marge might to tidy them, Roper's clothes looked bunched as burlap, ditch-colored, flecked with sticky seeds.

Doc had been the last one you'd expect to go like this, with all his skills and couth and looks. His dad a cardsharp, his mom a pianist, his superb digits a birthright. A dead loss now. Had we ever been fair to him? Had he volunteered to save those of us who stayed? or had we drafted him the second schoolkids made Marion go "Doc"? Roper's hands had left on us his best sort of signature: no trace of scar. All those binding little surgeries, ending with his Swiss-watch stitches, they'd long since gone invisible. For forty years, no need to put a © on any of his living creatures. Doc had tied the black catgut knot as he said: "No mark likely. You'll see. Good as new in no time, pal."

These few words still felt sure, short, as sunk clear into us as his sutures!

OF COURSE MARGE tried to get him carving again. Everybody did: "With all this water, bet you're *inspired*, huh?" Margie even risked the humiliation of buying him a Bobbitt's Hobby Shop napkin-ring kit. Maybe something simple would make him remember? But now only his own *fin*ished products drew him. Decoys. They were lures, okay.

Till the flood, simply *owning* had bored him. He'd told those big-spender Texans in Bermuda he cared nothing for buying; only *making* held him. Now he'd lost his talent for that, Doc Roper turned miser. He was a man fixed solely on gathering the work of one boy-wonder *Marion*! He'd become no better than any other of our country club's decoy-buyers. No better than me, than *I,* the poor bugger!

After forty years, Doc had left his job of saving us. All that huff-ing to warm a stethoscope, his personal-courtesy heat. That'd been Monday morning's first best medicine, lost. He'd left the healing task with no seeming regret. Even with all the forty-odd thank-you par-

ties in his honor, Roper had never given what you'd call a farewell-
speech. We did it all for him. He hadn't felt pressured to prepare a
different "Goodbye, I love you guys, too" for each big barbeque.

I would've. I probably might've written it out on three-by-fives
then memorized it so I could sound more . . . you know, more grandly
offhand . . . more, well, like *him*.

But, hey, Doc didn't *need* to endear. Man already had us all curled
right there in his hands. Talent! At base, its uneven distribution is so
unfair in a democracy.

Me? when *I* retired, my staff of five gave me one potted chrysan-
themum, a bottle of drugstore champagne, the giant greeting card
signed by our entire secretarial-and-paralegal team. Plus, "Hey, Bill,
can I help you tote that box of your desk stuff to your car? You
sure? Well, don't strain yourself right here at the end, guy. I mean
'at the starting-line.' Life's just getting cranked for you, you ole frat-
boy party-animal. Get out the hip flask and a list of 900 numbers."
(What *were* 900 numbers? I laughed, pretending to know.) Basically,
over and out. From an agency long ago renamed for me! No particular praise. Certainly no formal speech *about* me and, God knows, none
requested *from* me. Till now. Is *this* my own self-administered funeral
oration? Who else is left to give or hear it?

DOC HAD GONE on to reclaim, even dignify, his unfair handle
"Marion." Strapped with a liability, he made it famous. That's the
idea. That's American revenge!

Thanks to his old-school pull in medical circles years back, I'd
finally worked my way to the top of the list for a transplant. But
by now, see, I was too old to really qualify. I didn't "have the heart"
to claim an interchangeable human part, not when ruddy kids the
Bixbys' age lay waiting!

I could think to say that, sure, I'd loved Doc. I could say I had
wanted to *be* the man. But had I also wanted to, what? massage or
maybe "touch" or "ease" the fellow in some other way? Had I turned

that way? Had I, without knowing, become one of *those*—wearing their matching vest, tie and pocket hankie of the same priss-pot plaid? Was I another bachelor at another party gushing instead of speaking, making too much drama out of his dietetic childless life? Cute stories of his Yorkie's antics? Had I been miscast as husband-dad or maybe just faked it? Had I got myself rolled into Falls' city gates like the Trojan horse? himself a kind of decoy maybe. A wooden horse stuffed full of waiting warriors, male. Close quarters, beards, smells, a most macho silence.

I held on to the memory of a young doctor's clutching my hand so hard just after Dad died. Roper, tears in eyes already scarily blue, he'd squeezed my right paw while swearing that, having just let his patient slip off on the fairway, I would live forever-after in his care and hands. "I've *got* you, Bill!"

Who, except Doc, had ever promised that?

MAYBE I WANTED more. Had I wanted to "do it" with him or whatever? This is painful. There, I said it. But, really, where intimate contact with another male's concerned, I swear I wouldn't know how to go *about* it. Where would a fellow even start? A kiss? To kiss a mouth with stubble all around it? Nahh.

But even so, at my age, I'll admit to wanting *any*thing that might've once been true. (Whether I later re*mem*ber such a wish is quite another matter!) I know: I did hope for a bit more than I got. That is all I can now think to say.

With Doc finally downgraded into looking like some ole leather door hinge, I can maybe finally speak. But no longer actually *to* him, see? That chance appears lost. Odd but, for me, he doesn't even seem quite "old" yet. I still consider him all ages at once, since I myself seem to daily hopscotch across most of those same surplus annex decades.

But I confess that it was excellent—every year and day of our overlapping life spans—living just across the road from one another.

7

ONCE, A.D., I talked Jan into going for a country drive. Secretly I hoped to find a little property near some lake. A cabin maybe? Zero upkeep. Just let wildflowers grow. Nice porch.

But unlike Falls, devastation out there stayed uncleared. We passed flooded fields littered with Falls' refrigerators, house roofs, brand-new swing sets. The idea of enduring a deluge alone, no neighbor to fetch you off your roof, that sent us right back to our blank new place contented. Our condo still smells of drywall. So much the better.

Jan hates even going near our old neighborhood. "Nothing's down there but the river, a false friend." But I missed what I called "our lot in life": the mold-growing brick foundation where a mighty fortress stood for sixty years.

To even get near the place I must sneak the car keys now. Either my driving is getting worse or Jan's more critical or both.

THE FORMER PRETTIEST ride in eastern North Carolina now means ignoring the health department bulletins.

CONDEMNED OFF-LIMITS STRUCTURES, TRESPASSERS CONSIDERED LOOTERS. RAT BAIT POISON, DANGER TO UNLEASHED DOGS.

Oh it's a barrel of laughs down there these days. That badland border between Heaven and Hell must be riddled with just such vermin, smoke and signage.

Turning onto The River Road, I still feel a sort of quickening. Poor Janet can't even bear to see snapshots of our old place. But even the newish station wagon parks itself right where it should, the horse knows the way. Somehow, being here doesn't make me only sad.

I sit in our driveway and overlook the underpinnings of a house no longer here. Location, location, location, all that's left. Do you believe they still charge me property taxes? if at valuations greatly reduced. How fast Virginia creeper has claimed the north chimney, poison ivy's scaled the south.

At my wheel, arms crossed, I pose as Security. Some cocky boy-guard Colonel Paxton might've hired. But the kid's now minding the Old Mabry place. Like Doc, these days I feel my mission here is simply "looking."

Alone, I can admit that I have always been secretly insanely ambitious. But, for what? Shouldn't I know by now? Waiting, staring idled downriver, looking clear through what was Roper redwood deck, I spy a stretch of sandbank once public park. Its evergreen planting got swept away by current that first night. New saplings have taken root there. Mostly weed trees—sumacs and hackwoods. The river knits and braids along, all innocence. *Who, me?* after its rampage.

And I, here in my starter position as father-husband-neighbor, I do hope the police will come with questions. I'm spoiling for a challenge from far younger men. That way I can show my license—1526 River Road still written on it bold. Parked here, with no pressing business appointments, I try recovering whatever Riverside I liked best. This is a luxury peculiar to my age. The living and the dead make up your quorum and are all on call.

So I go back, before marriage, pre-ownership, to my much-missed Red, his introductory-offer. We're a family, back before Paxton gave us our free pass.

Dad's tour of the stars' homes commenced as soon as Sunday service ended. I would claim the Studebaker's flannel backseat. We had just worshipped at Second Methodist, while guiltily considering buying up toward First Presbyterian. Red pulled past First to check out how many new cars it had. And for Episcopalianism? That might only be achieved in our next generation.

At preachers' last Amen, town believers scattered, starved. Bound for delicious-smelling home roasts; to reservations at Chez Josephine or Sanitary Seafood. But Dad, unswerving, aimed the waxed red Studebaker riverward. Our lunch budget might prove limited. (Chicken salad sandwiches today featuring a hen past steady laying.) Even so, a grand tour awaited.

Studebaker whitewalls? Dad had Cloroxed those as clean as Astaire's spats. Strangers, we took The River Road's first S-curve. Leaving much of summer's heat behind, we soon banked, cooling and downhill, past yonder little vest-pocket park.

There, Red (the boy) had made a French picnic from two hard-boiled eggs. And now, with the doxology fresh behind us, he called to order truest worship. "Will you lookeee at all this back up in here?" Red asked us and the world generally. *Enter into His gates with thanks-giving, His courts with praise.*

Their houses already looked beautiful to us. Lawns stretched too wide to be anything but show-off meadows. Beyond those, vertical homes, caulked with fresh face-paint, lined like beauties about to be confirmed. Striped awnings trapped coolness back of second-story window. Homes soon appeared almost a single sawtoothed stage-set, painted just so. For luring humbler folk right down into this river shade.

That Sunday mid-July, home-places of the rich all seemed only made of shady porches, steep foyers. Once you stepped over welcome mats, would there even be a place to sit or sleep? Such beautiful Victorian valentines, homes might prove depthless as birdhouses.

But us? we'd not get far enough indoors to check. We'd just enjoy the sight of carpet yards. We could enjoy our safety, being hicks out on a public road. From here, such places looked lovely as all promises well-kept.

Why had riverfront-living so spoken to the bowlegged contractor driving us? Red wanted it for us. That Sabbath, he chugged along at twelve mph. Dad pointed out heart-shaped goldfish ponds, the engineering of a Queen Anne turret. And I, in his backseat, slouched ever-lower.

None of my country classmates would see us ogling here. But

our car already drew smirks from neighbor girls on bikes. They were beauties wearing shorts. They had hair so blond, it wasn't even yellow like our best farm girls'. Here, it shone toward a silver that no store-bought home-slopped dye could fake.

I saw girls as pretty as girls should ever legally get to be this side of intentional international torture of such farm boys as Dad and me! But why were they wearing short-shorts on the Lord's Day? And why outdoors, goofing around at this post-church Sabbath-dinner-hour? Their smiling at our poker-faced tourism made me wince like some-one burned. I felt a mixture: pity for myself, desire for them, and one huge secret wish not unlike Dad's. Did I want to live among them or punish them from afar for their vanity and luck and legs? '

But he was hollering into his rearview mirror, "Set up straight, son. Show 'em that posture. Gals your age're out here grinning a big River Road greetings. Gals sure get 'developed' fast in town. And you? scrunched-down a-hiding! Sit *up*. You're a good-looking whip-persnap. You covering your face!? Why, if I'd of had your looks . . . I might could have got somewheres with our life. —See yonder? Since laist week the Eatman Battles have had a whole new flagstone ter-race laid. Leading to their dock. Probably fine Dovetail Construction work. It just appreciates their property value. Like I always say, 'Why not en*joy* your money?' Imagine, son. Your bike would be parked alongside our own house. Your Sunfish boat, the sails up, docked out back! How'd you like them apples, hunh, Billy?"

"Yessir," I droned. Glad there was no hope. Of Pop ever getting what he swore we all deserved. Meanwhile, behind us, six cars, two of them Packards, pressed closer trying to finally pass. Good taste alone kept them from honking us off the road.

And only now, from this far riverbank, only while recalling Dad's tour of all he wanted for us, do I see why Riverside summers stayed so cool. It had more than just the shading lid of maples, more than just the mild river itself.

Earlier we'd driven through hot farmland, flat and glaring. We were now headed down, down a slow grade into the only river chasm hereabouts. No wonder wetness kept things here a bright currency-green. This road along a river was incised below sea-level. This wide avenue eased us right down into moisture, a beautiful gash or trench. Fill this with water? you're done for. All your property's in the Panama Canal. And the Mabrys' life wish?

To be allowed to settle exactly here.

They put out the bait. It brought us.

8

SIX MORE DAMAGED "Marions" had been retrieved. One they found washed as far as Greenville, thirty-four miles, carried over all that flooded farmland. It was a mallard, cleaved down the exact center; but still it floated, bobbing weirdly sunny-side up. Its swamp-soaked bill, back-curved, made the bird appear to smile. Had it gone smug (or crazed) with everything it'd seen?

—Myself, I am an optimist, about nothing.

Because Doc engraved his Internet-registered name into his creations' bottoms, others would get returned that whole next year. (One from South Carolina's Great Pee Dee River but folks traced its carver here to Falls.)

Marge kept him nested in, secreted away right down our street. Riding past, Jan and I, we'd sometimes catch sight of her cutting his hair on their side patio. Doc's head bent so far forward he looked about to fall as he sat wrapped in a checked tablecloth. The old man seemed irked at suffering such grooming, her free hand held his noggin still.

Margie's gaunt now but ever more vigilant and butch. Odd, she looks more bowlegged. Her hair's chopped short any old way. (Being so on-guard for two, she finds no beauty-parlor time. "A shame," Jan says. "Time-off would do her a world of good, hearing others' little troubles.") Still, Marge's always been so basically fine-looking, she's never needed much sissy-tending.

The Ropers' back-door Hilltop neighbors, the Blanchards, who had lost their cat and almost their granddaughter, swear that Doc often sleeps alone in his old tobacco-colored pup tent pitched far up under their back deck, for further privacy.

SOMETIMES SHE'LL DRIVE him clear out of town where they're sure to meet no concerned friends. She parks while he basically "looks," as the Ropers both agree to call it. Marge keeps him in sight but all while simply settled at the wheel, reading that day's Raleigh paper, flossing, talking to her kids by phone, listening to oldies or Public Radio.

She said that when a couple of his carvings started returning by mail as if via their own will, the sight of ruined ones went harder on Doc. Simpler to believe his waterbirds were somehow "gone." Migratory, off to seek their fortunes, looking flag-perfect as his decoys did when starting out.

I found it sad but enviable, Marge's daily carpooling him someplace new. I offered to be her driver stand-in. She thanked me with the saddest smile. "By now, he trusts nobody but me. Not even you, Bill. And we both know, that's saying a lot."

"Appreciate that, Marge." I lowered my eyes, too grateful.

He needed motion, daily hunting. Instead of dawn river-swims, he took to this striding. She'd drive him out still farther and farther. Had he ever told her what he hoped to find? Did his wife dare ask? Theirs proved such a marriage, "in sickness and in health." A thing now grown unto itself. Beautiful how patient, how simply she lived inside the damage done to him. *Now, that's a love story*, I thought, not bothering Janet by my saying it aloud. Somehow that'd sound critical of *her*. —Roper-marriage comparisons, even now!

If Margie got home ten minutes late from grocery shopping, she confessed to sometimes finding he'd stolen off "to go look." This proved pretty dangerous. See, Doc's route stayed fixed along our county's old waterways. Thanks to city planners and prosperity, many tributaries have been trained through exurban infrastructure, pipes and aqueducts. Lithium, it's been sent grave-deep, giving us no surface balm. Clear springs where a decoy or some live bird could splash? all imprisoned underground. Streams might bubble up across some unzoned field only to plunge blind, back under the interstate.

But Doc, following the old brook with a dowser's nose, barely noticed. He mostly stared down. The man seemed unaware of new highways' barricading wetlands' way. Being a former Boy Scout (Eagle!) —how literally he mapped a stream! The man and his stick walked right through (then out of) any brook-straddling dress shop at a sudden tony mall, startling security.

THE RISKS ROPER trailed everywhere, he alone never saw. The man never actually looked back: as Doc's former patients kept pulling their cars over, wanting to help. No time for signaling, folks just veered off-road to offer, what? cash? Starbucks? rides home? He had taught us how to breathe wet kids alive while out for his jog. He had heart-massaged a dead man twenty bonus-minutes extra just in case. His rescuer's impulse came back and schooled us all. We each longed for the right and privilege of finding him horizontal so we might just once work on *him*. However badly.

But even if some former patient hollered, sprung out of his car, blocked the old guy's path, Doc would shake his head no. Cornered, he'd fight you. His wooden staff laid quite a dent into the hood of co-Olympic-gold-medalist Tomothy Bixby's new red Miata. Finally, the unscarred folks that Doc had left "as good as new" were forced to give up sparing *him*. Safer for us all, just leaving him endangered. He seemed everywhere, replicas.

Out driving myself, I had the mixed luck of spotting him. Wanting to help I cringed instead. Then risked a few wild U-turns to hurry anyplace else. He had looked . . . feral. What would I even *say*? I felt a traitor to my early starstruck sense of him. Roper'd promised to keep me alive and, till this sec at least, hadn't he? But seeing him so publicly addled seemed a gentling hint to let myself go now. Permission. A hall pass.

Part of me longed to join my mentor in his roadside quest. Hike beside him, pointing, "Great to be out looking with you. But, uh-oh, bud, we missed a ditch." And yet, this short of breath, I couldn't have kept up with his long blue-heron strides. Even if he'd ever finally invited me.

Janet begged that I stop taking out the car alone. She made me get one of those emergency beepers. You wear it around your neck 24–7. Cowbell. This way I could summon 911 without even needing the digital skill to dial three numbers. "Having fallen, simply press red button," instructions state. But *why?*

Jan suddenly claimed she loved riding shotgun with me, even if I was headed off to buy spare lightbulbs. Monitoring, pure and simple. I knew she kept nitroglycerin ampules in her handbag. And the cell phone? given my state, she now carried hers from room to room. Subtle. I just needed one hour alone per day. Too much to ask at my age? I recalled first being stared at by Jan with me sitting unzipped, grade three. And, for better or worse, my unsentimental friend had never stopped, never looked at anyone else.

She feared my next "episode" might crash me into other cars. Every nearby vehicle seemed to contain her ideal young family, ourselves forty years ago. My bad driving and worse heart had become the enemy of precisely us.

"Episodes." Getting closer together. Contractions, hints. Dilations of egress by centimeters, signs that some canal way out of the world was finally clearing. Last month at a mall shoe store, after buying nice new fleece slippers, I dropped my receipt. As I bent to grab it, their white carpet started looking so good, contrasting with the cold air up at usual six-foot adult male level, I went down to be more toward flooring's weave.

Perfect bed, placed exactly where Daddy presently needed one. Janet insisted I had fallen. I later vowed to her: It had not been an actual fall. More that I simply eased lower, by degree, toward floor covering of increasing interest. Once achieved, the horizontal there felt very valuable indeed.

Young clerks refused to let me enjoy it long. First I heard them above me barking at each other, "You check. Touch his neck or wherever they do, and see. No, you. You've got seni*o*rity." I had to laugh at this. Relieved, they jumped, then swore. "Oh . . . ma . . . God. Well, good. The paperwork alone! And already it's been such a week!"

Despite my explanations of what a great floor surface they had going here, the kids would just not let me keep admiring it up close. The prettiest girl drove me home. She then led me across the deck, into our house. I don't know why the sight of Janet's stricken face made me cackle so. Did Jan imagine I was finally bringing home the reason for my live-in absence all these years, my mistress-nurse age 22? That gave me a momentary giggling power surge. Till, weirdly strong, the two of them lifted me right onto the bed.

ON DAYS I feel very clear and able, I still try and sneak her car keys. Sounds like some juvenile delinquent with his greaser's ducktail. Making the big bank-heist getaway in a two-year-old Volvo wagon! But look, these days I go barely twelve mph. Like Dad as self-appointed docent to Riverside's top mansions. People honk at me, I go so slow, which is good. Keeps me more alert. Jan'll be standing at our community mailboxes or talking by phone to Marge (in lowered tones about lessening expectations for their men), and me? I'm just then rolling downhill in neutral. Sly, my Steve McQueen exit strategy! Go un-noisy into that dark night . . . I've grown into one cunning pioneering "Red" old man.

I tend to drive along the ragged marsh edges of Mall World. That coincidentally is where Doc mostly hikes now. I tell myself I am somehow using my aloneness to protect him and his. I plan guarding him with whatever's least likely to bother Doc as he is now.

Marge tried restricting him to the strip mall nearest our development. But even old men are hard to contain. I just want to see him. Whatever he keeps seeking, I sense he's now pursuing that for me. Or is it me he's half-forgotten and now absently seeks? Even in ditches, minor sinkhole graves.

It's counterproductive, living in a town so small. Limits your escaping unobserved. More new charismatic churches, while car dealerships keep closing, and no Harley-Davidson outlet for the Fallen. So small a place when one has hopes so Roper-huge. And, what did I *want* for him and myself? That . . . that's on the tip of my tongue. It's just, to me, the two of us always seemed secretly made of finer stuff. Alike in being different. But what chance did we have, in a zone so rural, strict and married?

It's hard to spot my dearest wanderer-friend outdoors and in such public need. What's tougher still? Not seeing him at all!

Anybody hereabouts can tell you—and for years—why I'd have done just anything for Roper.

9

DRIVING CALMS ME. Hands around the wheel, I briefly forget my own factory-second arteries. For miles I ignore even Doc's splintery mind. I like the Swedish clicking of my turn signal. He'll sometimes suddenly appear. Along roadside, you'll see him scare certain schoolkids holding signs for their booster-club car wash.

Last month I spied him way off in the distance. He kept prodding the bank of some irrigation pond. Doc, following his stick, came wading its shoreline silhouetted. He looked like both a ragged crane and some homeless Audubon, hunting all that he'd so slowly painted, then too quickly lost.

A few locals freely talk of getting up a petition. They've urged Marge to ship our shaman-friend off somewhere. "For help." Light-dosage shock-therapy is back in fashion: a flash of lightning might offset his head full of goose down and black water.

They claim Roper is now "sending the wrong signal to Falls' newcomers." Among drinkers at Hole Nineteen, I actually heard our Republican mayor, one of Doc's former patients, explain how the man has become "both a traffic nuisance and eyesore."

Everybody says that life is short and yet it's highly possible to overstay.

Take me. Please! Surely our "best if used by" dates, Doc's and mine, have themselves by now retired to Bermuda! Maybe he and I are twinned, even in this. On principle I favor elective mercy-killing if the patient's clear and perfectly ready. Surely a human right.

—Still I keep waiting for some sleep-inducing hypo warmed by breath, some pink-slip prescription: "Please excuse Bill permanently from Phys. Ed. and, far as that goes, from Phys. Send him instead to Library Study Hall forever." Meanwhile, Doc searches.

AFTER YEARS SPENT succeeding far from home, Roper's children have started coming back. Jan and I, we'll lately notice the daughter or sometimes the boy out walking their dad.

And I, being around more due to certain congestive setbacks not worth recording here, chanced to stand watching the street from our new sunporch. Magazines now bore me. True, we keep the Raleigh *News & Observer* going, but we've unsubscribed from *Time*. At our age, everything piles up so.

I called to Janet one room away and quizzed her. If *all* our neighbors' kids return for regular visits, why do the Roper kids' delayed trips stand out? Oldsters on our block speak of Doc's kids as extra-saintly, flying south so much here lately. We even saw the rangy theologian, up a tall ladder, installing his parents' storm windows. He kept having to wave at the parade of interested older cars.

Janet, her hands coated in Christmas baking flour, said, "What?" then, chin on my shoulder, leaned half against me. We studied Doc and Marge's daughter. Arms crossed, this pale young woman simply waited. Eyes half-shut in sunlight, she stood at the curb. I pointed, "What, she's going more platinum?"

"Get your eyes rechecked. It's white. She's nearly fifty, Billy. The children all are. My rule of thumb, add twenty years to everyone, that usually comes out about right."

"White!" I said.

Doc's daughter let him explore. Bushes and curbs, at his own pace. She just minded our general practitioner, his sitter today.

"Maybe we notice," Janet guessed, "because she's finally coming home to doctor *him*? Could be that's why his kids fight to take their turns now. Coast clear. Doc's forgot to show he's too independent to need anybody's help. —His girl looks easy enough doing it, doesn't she? Like she has all the time in the world. It was the last thing her old man forgot. But he's finally stopped saying no."

Listening, nodding, without any reason, I wanted to cry. Had Jan meant to make me? —Cheap emotions seem unlike us. Me.

Looking out, I did manage, "Patient child. —Still quite pretty. She got his eyes."

IO

THIS IS THE end, come all of a sudden at last. You will be almost as glad for it as I. Oh, and thank you for sticking with me through this hell and high water. Between paradise and the tar pit there must be quite a violent border ahead, passport-issues.

During my whole life I've never said so much at once as in this thinking-dreaming-recall-chant, last thing. Being one who's stayed, I'm trying to find the balance needed now for traveling. Like that liquid metal Doc funneled last thing into his carvings' undersides. To keep birds upright on their shelf or steadied in black water.

Finally what I've most wanted and feared finds me like an honor. Why bother trying to prepare for our own good deaths? We'll each know how. At least, well enough to finally get 'er done. And, if we "choke"? Well, all the better.

—I was driving, see, to buy skim milk, plus cuttlebones for those immortal cockatiels. I'd just invented this chore. Told myself it mattered, might produce a small adventure. Help justify my stealing dear Jan's car keys one more time.

You know that juncture near the new mall where beggars haunt our medians? They'll try and clean your car window. Red-haired, smoking cigs, big beer guts, they wear khaki, pretending they're retired military. CONFUSED BUSH SAND-WAR VET WILL STILL WORK. But they leave smudges so you have to pay to get *those* cleared. They try to snag folding money from older fellows like me. (Democrat though I am, these guys really burn me up.) I spied one up ahead hiking fast a full yard into my lane. I let myself honk. Felt good to. His overcoat was army surplus, the stride rolled forward, lanky, deliberate. Rearview alone showed his shepherd's staff.

I pull right over, no time for signaling. Dead ahead of Doc, I angle, waiting. Last-thing I'll try and trap him. Straight ahead, the sunset's quite a blaze. Red taillights lead that way and irritate it. Sinking sun shows a sky like golden sand piled with ruby mountains halfway through some mad spin cycle. My windshield's smeared with undeserved pastels. Janet has been vigilant all day keeping me "grounded." I thought she'd never nod off, needlepointing her OLD AGE AIN'T FOR SISSIES pillow slip. (Poor ole sissies must age, too.)

He hurtles along this dangerous commercial stretch. He staffs along his wild clear energy. Traffic shoots around him; cars keep honking, going sixty-easy in a zone marked forty-five.

I've parked poorly, too near an open ditch. My left arm curves around the steering wheel; I throw the right along seat-back. Where *is* he? A flashing ambulance veers wide of him. The driver's screaming, "Fool!"

Feeling breathless, waiting, I've buzzed our passenger window down. Ready for the coot, I'm hunched forward to stop my friend. But I keep hearing the car engine or maybe some tire acting up, stray whumping knocks. Only now do I study my chest. The ole ticker's just a-pounding. My white shirtfront literally shifts forward-back. Not real good of a personal sign, I guess. Seeing a passing stick, I shout, "Doc! Yer ole Bill here. Need a lift?" No answer. I start screaming, "Help me, *help* me, sir!"

The figure halts. I see a body bend, look in. I note how creased the face. Moon-cracked, it fills my window. The head cocks. I see an expression half-known. If I'd only somehow stayed this man's familiar.

"*Bill* here, Doc. No sweat. Crawl in. Boy, have I missed you. Remember when we were like brothers? Remember Dad's dying, trusting us like that? Just me here, your Bill, sir. Needin' help for sure. See, nobody knows the trouble or what to *do* with me these days. —Ideas, pal?"

I POINT AT my own pounding chest. He looks. Doc really looks. Then my right hand shoots his way, "Put her *there*, pardner!" Stupid thing to try. Trick him into touching me once more.

He swings back, skull hitting window-frame. I'd just been hoping for a final borrowed spark.

Traffic passes. Where are they all *going*? My paw feels cold, exposed in air between us. Sunset keeps candy-tinting everything. He gapes at my extended hand.

Then I see him notice: recent dark lesions biting into its back. He appears, if not concerned, at least still scientific.

"Well, *look* at you." A dry old voice husks Roper's deeper wetter first one. His hands have both lost weight: now spindles, needles, sinew. He says directly to my hand, "Bill's liver spots . . . more sunken now."

Doc bows through open car window, the stick propped outside. My beloved helper touches me. In that touch I swear I feel a father's card-sense, the Mom's Chopin, and Yale. He turns my wrist his way. He scans whatever one hand's backside shows. From his palm's heat I get the smallest splash.

My doctor, best on earth, is reading me alive again! Imagine. He studies newer dents. He's judging how blue veins now weave to the surface. In golden light Doc shifts the old mitt, reaches down along its wrist. Fingertips seeking my pulse. Tickles. I cannot explain the relief. Just to have been touched. Interest is healing.

Doc's lips move. He's counting beats, my vital signs. His eyes slide west where they can linger, tally, private. Traffic whizzes wide of us. Wind keeps moving his crazed hair. Eyes narrow their pouches. He gazes my way, but as if across some vast marsh. Roper's eyes, always a strong blue, appear electrocuted several shades brighter. Leery. Senile only? Maybe burned clear back to his startled bartering youth.

"This ole Bill I'm seeing? Is, right? Bit confused here. That still you, son?"

"Yes, sir."

"But where'd you go, 'Mondays, six forty-five a.m.'? Started out our weeks right, 'member? But, there was a flood, you know. Is this really Red's Billy? Looks like time's messed you up pretty good, huh? Tough deal all-round. As for your having pulse, son . . . ?"

I simply nod, eyebrows up as invitation.

"Well, hell, Bill, boy. Nobody's been taking *care* of you. Probably said *I* would. But, being up this age, I keep tellin' 'em—just can't *do* it all anymore."

"But you, Doc, *you're* still moving!"

"Hopping, more like. Frog legs in the skillet. No. For all practical purposes, professionally-speaking, son? the two of us we're *dead*! Hate to be the one telling you. No, maybe best it's me. Fact is you got no vital signs to mention. Reflexes're all that's left us. Surprised she even let you have the car. Goners, the both of us."

"Well, thank you. See, nobody would *tell* me. You know, all along I felt we . . . I always wished we could've . . . But, didn't we have *fun*?"

"Had the *what*?" His hearing's shot. Doc releases my hand, all but throws it back at me. Everything cools further. The man ducks out backward. He's already upright, moving, his staff fast-forwarding along more ditch, crackling weeds ahead. Again he has forgotten me. No backward-sideways glance. But that's okay.

Now I can lower my right hand, right? Can simply press it to my slamming rib cage. I finally know. I've heard it from the best. If I breathe now it is to count the few breaths he predicted. Very big adventure slated incoming, sir.

Car ignition purrs as I direct my front-tires a foot more off tarmac but overshoot. With one thudding metal shriek-thud, my whole front seat topples right.

Car's tipped pretty good into the drainage-ditch. Sun keeps sinking over our second-best mall. Sunset's going nowhere fast. Looks like skyline there wants only to go back toward perfect wilderness again. Before golf, pre-farms, prior to people, even Tuscarora ones, when creatures lived here unmonitored and whole. That's what I want and where I seek. Any minute now. The rest.

I note my blinkers going. Cocked off-road here, help's unlikely. Falls? all new people. Gone those days when any kid falling off his bike brought Band-Aid strangers out of beautiful homes. Half now from Mexico City, the rest pure Jersey City, nice-enough total-strangers. Among the Fallen who chose to stay, few my age have managed staying put. Nobody to recognize my car. No one to know my fluky heart, my true friend, my Red, my country club connection, my loves, love . . .

Still, we did just talk. Among our best conversations, at least our most efficient. And he was telling me . . . ? oh yes, that "we must remember to be dead now." *Houston? Phase III achieved at last.* Note to self: High-time you hightail it, Ducktail.

Once he swore, "I've *got* you, Bill." Now, not. Catch-and-release. We're all wildlife. Basically, it's all catch-and-release.

JAN WILL WAKE over her needlework, phone the cops. "He's out again, boys." Still, that gives me time aplenty to take care of business, leave the building. I've got this ugly plastic dog tag at my throat. Aren't necklaces effeminate? Punch its red button, they'll swarm in on me. But no, at last I have the needed information. From the only one on earth who'd know then tell. So few such men. To be recognized, diagnosed, dismissed, and nearly-blessed. Who'd dare ask more?

That single young male wood duck is still Doc's finest. Something about its cockiness, crest. My wished last mission: collecting that. Doc and I, we never needed to say much. Between buddies, a whole whole lot went understood.

—Pleased to now go drifting. Safe from any sternum-busting code-blue. Didn't crash her car into a perfect young family. Promised Janet that, at least. We're up-to-date, God bless her long patience with me. Shouldn't have monopolized someone so good. Could've run any multinational, that one.

Hammocked here behind safety belt, I will want to go and hunt the boy-one naturally. Woody the Wood Duck, son of Red. A flotation device I myself could not have carved. His masterpiece, a sort of portrait of me, know it or not. He always saw so much in me. Too much?

("Hardly a pulse," he said. You know, I *thought* there was a problem.)

I TRUST SEATBELT to hold me half up. Nodding, I hear his sensible order, "Align. Head. Please." Obeying, I feel clarity return. Soon I'm finding a horizon I've kept aiming for since farm life. Car's not even needed now (some larval stage abandoned). Now my old gray space opens to more liquid time. I seem on-water, am Tomothy Timothy Bixby—amphibious. Alone and somehow setting out by rowboat, so . . . gunwales creak, two battered oars. Ocean current's basically in charge. Evening alone on the water. Fine by me, though chill. Should've brought my windbreaker. Out here somewhere, just offshore, my simple stand-in bobs. Daring me to find him, teasing.

His carver knew me pretty well. I want art's findings now and have come to collect. This was my own long ago, and how can that be wrong? I somehow sense my trophy just ahead. So much dark water, little ruddering's now possible. Day is giving way. Passing the little docks, I see lamps switching on in beachfront family homes. Sunset wicks up all the blues into one red soon turned thorough black. Shadows keeping mashing down on darkness even blacker. And over water, over me, stars brighten till they each have fur. Male, most stars. The search is long and I have lost one oar but, among yet another brace of reeds, touch alone tells me I am near it.

Here, now, this. Finally my very own one, actually my first. For keeps, too. How easily and wet it comes to me. Un-shy if silver-cold to touch. Darkness helps me feel its sides' engraving, every feather's cut as strict as Bible braille. Not one mistake, no faking. It bulks here in my hands. Made just for me, made almost *as* me. Since I've lacked my own fuller version, I'll trust his one of me just that much more.

Tonight its weight feels excellent, exact as the mystery of being male. It rests safe here in my lap. Air's turned colder, salted, But thanks to this loss returned, I swear I feel sum-totaled. Fear no evil in me, ever. Oh I know this is just a carving. Not an actual life. (But, did I even half-deserve another person, a whole splendid extra one of those and just for me?)

BOY, BUT NIGHT comes down so hard around our little boat.

I cling to this object, man-made. Still, I knew the man made it. Seems, what? Confused. There's just one thing I've forgot to do. What? But wasn't that the agreement? I was either meant to *be* or *love* him . . . Cannot for the life of me remember which. At least he kindly sent me out with this. Sure seemed to think the world of me. And yet, I . . . what? I go.

A man accompanied. A man one certain other worthy man described.

See, that is why I value this.
See, that is why I've waited.

ACKNOWLEDGMENTS

WRITERS NEED READERS while the inkjet lettering's still warm. I am honored to thank my own responsive, candid friends: Jane Holding, Elizabeth Spencer, Diana Ricketts, Paul Taylor, Joanne Meschery, Cecil Wooten, Danny Kaiser, Erica Eisdorfer, David Deming, Shirley Drechsel, Chuck Adams, Charles Millard, Alan Shapiro, Mona Simpson, Sam Stephenson, Will Menaker, Katie Adams, Dave Cole, Ret. District Court Judge Patricia Devine, therapist Bob Vaillancourt, computer therapist Paul Rosenberg, Nancy Demorest and Bruce Gurganus. Dr. Jess Peter, cardiac advisor to certain of my characters, helped me diagnose the imaginary.

My agent, Amanda Urban, has shown both loving discernment and rare patience with my perfectionism or whatever it is.

I am especially happy to acknowledge my new editor, Robert Weil. His affectionate respect for my work first brought me to Liveright. May this be the first of many books to emerge under Bob Weil's scrupulous, imaginative care.

Time is the greatest gift. For that, I stand indebted to the John Simon Guggenheim Foundation. The Lannan Foundation and the Corporation of Yaddo each took me in, offering a block of clear time. This book is the byproduct of gratitude.

Thank you, friends. And thank you, readers.